A RACE OF TRIALS

A Shade of Vampire, Book 35

Bella Forrest

D1707325

ALSO BY BELLA FORREST:

A SHADE OF DRAGON:

A Shade of Dragon 1
A Shade of Dragon 2
A Shade of Dragon 3

BEAUTIFUL MONSTER DUOLOGY:

Beautiful Monster 1
Beautiful Monster 2

A SHADE OF KIEV TRILOGY:

A Shade of Kiev 1
A Shade of Kiev 2
A Shade of Kiev 3

For an updated list of Bella's books,
please visit www.bellaforrest.net

Join my VIP email list and I'll personally send you an email reminder as
soon as my next book is out!
Click here to sign up: www.forrestbooks.com

Contents

THE "NEW GENERATION" NAMES LIST

- **Arwen:** (daughter of Corrine and Ibrahim - witch)
- **Benedict:** (son of Rose and Caleb - human)
- **Brock:** (son of Kiev and Mona – half warlock)
- **Grace:** (daughter of Ben and River – half fae and half human)
- **Hazel:** (daughter of Rose and Caleb – human)
- **Heath:** (son of Jeriad and Sylvia – half dragon and half human)
- **Ruby:** (daughter of Claudia and Yuri – human)
- **Victoria:** (daughter of Vivienne and Xavier – human)

Hazel

I woke up once again to the misty orange sky of Nevertide.

My parents still thought we were enjoying a vacation on Murkbeech Island, not playing deadly games to win our freedom. I wondered how long it would take for them to discover that we were missing, and what they would—or, heck, could—do to find us. We still had no idea where this mysterious land was located.

Tejus had gone early this morning to talk with the ministers, no doubt to discuss the progression of the trials. The last one had gone horribly wrong, resulting in the deaths of three sentries and many more injured. Had it not been for Tejus, there would have been many more. We still

1

didn't know who was responsible for the disaster.

I dreaded what lay ahead. It wasn't just me I was worried for—it was Ruby and the boys too. The threat of Jenus might have been laid to rest, but I didn't trust anyone in the kingdom. Only a few days ago, a cloaked figure had tried to kidnap me from the castle, right from Tejus's quarters where I was meant to be safe, and we still hadn't discovered the culprit.

Looking around the empty, silent room, I suddenly had a yearning to see my friends.

Though I had promised not to, I headed for the door to leave Tejus's living quarters. The 'human' quarters where Ruby, Benedict and Julian were staying were located in the belly of Hellswan castle, which was well-guarded—as the trials progressed, we humans had become a much more valuable commodity. After the kidnapping attempt, Tejus had insisted that I stayed permanently with him in his quarters until the trials were over, defying my wishes to join the others.

I made my way swiftly through the castle, surprising myself. I was actually getting to know some of its winding passages and nondescript hallways, which all seemed to work against simple navigation. One looked very much like another, so it was nearly impossible to pinpoint where you were. The idea that I was becoming familiar with it depressed me—clearly we had spent too long inside its imposing gray walls.

At the wide double doors of the human quarters, I came to an abrupt halt and looked up at the two guards standing outside. Both were heavily armed, but they recognized me. With silent nods of acknowledgement, they moved aside and let me through.

"Hazel!" Ruby stood up from the breakfast table and rushed over to me, wrapping me in a warm, familiar hug. Julian was too busy stuffing his face with fruit to do more than wave, and Benedict just looked sleepily over at me, his eyelids drooping. He'd never been much of a morning person, but this excessively tired state was unusual even for him.

"Are you okay?" I asked him.

"Me?" He looked bewildered. "I'm fine. Why wouldn't I be?"

I shrugged. I was probably being overly concerned.

I eyed the breakfast table with amusement. The food looked good—better than what was provided for the Hellswan royalty and dignitaries. Clearly being Ash's champion had its advantages.

"Have you heard anything about the next trial?" Ruby

asked.

"No, not yet. Tejus has gone to talk to the ministers," I replied. "I guess we'll find out later."

"Ash has gone too," Ruby said.

I sat down at one of the numerous spare seats around the table—there was enough space and food here to feed an entire army. I picked at a piece of cheese, too nervous to have much of an appetite.

"Hazel." Ruby observed me. "If you don't eat more than that, you're not going to be much help to anyone." She poured me a strange-colored juice and piled some fruit on my plate.

I grinned at her. "We're on opposite teams, remember? You should be encouraging my weakened state."

"It's so *weird*," Benedict said. "Why can't you both just help Ash? Then you could stay with us, Hazel."

Ruby and I glanced at one another. We'd made the decision to do this—to each champion a different sentry in the kingship trials to increase our chances of getting out of Nevertide and back to The Shade. But yes, it would have been good if I'd been able to stay here with them. Instead, I was relegated to the bolt-hole of mystical energy crystals that Tejus still asked me to sleep in to increase my mental energy so he could milk it… I guessed I knew now

4

what it felt like to be a cow.

"You know why we're doing it," I said.

"We'd better hope that Tejus keeps his word to let you go if he wins," Benedict muttered.

"Yes, I believe he will," I replied. I trusted Tejus to keep his word, and I trusted him over Ash— perhaps just because I'd spent more time with Tejus. As strange as it seemed, Tejus and I had grown closer as we overcame the countless hurdles that Nevertide seemed to be throwing our way. It felt perplexing to be planting ourselves on opposite sides, but Ruby and I were doing the right thing. It was the best we could do in our dire situation.

"Well, I don't," Julian burst out. "I think we've spent too long helping the sentries with their stupid trials—and it's about time that we actually tried to figure a way out of here on our *own*."

"We *have* tried," Ruby replied. "The barriers are up, remember? And it's going to take a power greater than the four of us to get them back down again."

I agreed with Ruby. We didn't have a hope in hell without a witch or warlock, and I had yet to see one in Nevertide. The trials were our only chance of getting back home. Julian's outburst surprised me though; I'd thought we were all behind this plan, but evidently not.

"I don't think they're going to be as deadly as the first trial," I said, thinking that perhaps fear for my and Ruby's safety was behind his frustration. "That was a mistake—someone had tampered with the disk."

"And we don't know who," Julian shot back, "so what's stopping them from doing it again?"

"Tejus is back in the running. I think we'll be safer with him around," I replied, although I knew my argument sounded weak.

Julian was right. We hadn't found the person responsible for meddling in the first trial, and there would be nothing to stop them from doing it again.

"Don't you think it's convenient," Julian continued, "that Tejus was out of the trials till he managed to *save the day*, and now he's been reinstated?"

I chewed my lip. I knew what Julian was insinuating—that Tejus had something to do with the faulty disk, but I couldn't bring myself to believe that. Tejus was not exactly high up on my best friend list, but he seemed honorable… I couldn't picture him stooping *that* low. That was something Jenus would have done.

Julian slumped back in his seat, still frustrated, but apparently willing to let the matter slide for now.

I looked over at Benedict. He hadn't said a word

throughout the exchange, and looked as if he were close to falling asleep in his porridge. I was about to continue talking quietly to Ruby, when the guards swung open the front doors and Tejus strode into the room.

His dark eyes found me instantly, as if none of the others even existed.

"Come, Hazel. I've heard news about the trials."

Good morning to you too.

Sighing, I rose to my feet. "I'll see you later, guys…" I glanced around the table, my focus settling on my sleepy brother. "Benedict, you should get some rest."

He nodded wearily.

Ruby gave me a brief hug goodbye, and then I trailed off behind Tejus as he began his brisk walk back up the tower to his living quarters.

"So what did you learn?" I asked as I trotted to keep up.

"Not here," he replied shortly.

As soon as we entered the hallway that led to his rooms, Lucifer, his moody feline, crept up and started winding his sleek body around our legs. Clearly I'd gained some sort of acceptance with the creature.

Tejus ignored him and didn't drop his pace until we reached his living room. Letting both Lucifer and me inside, he slammed the door and locked it.

He motioned for me to sit down on one of the velvet-covered sofas while he walked over to the windows and resumed his habitual position, staring out across the kingdoms—a sign I was beginning to understand meant something was bothering him.

I observed his profile as I waited patiently for him to speak—the towering and well-built frame, the Roman nose, the shadowed, deep-set eyes and long, dark brown hair that was tied at the nape of his neck. He wore his warrior's uniform of black shirt and loose silk trousers, along with the black robe that he adopted whenever he was due to meet with royal officials. Tejus no longer intimidated me in the same way he had when we'd first met, but objectively his presence was an unsettling one. I couldn't imagine Ash, or anyone else for that matter, coming up against him in the trials and winning.

"They have all been reinstated," Tejus murmured without looking at me, "all those at the first trial. Three passed away, another dropped out of their own volition."

"How many are there now?" There had been quite a few at the first trial, men and women from all over Hellswan who were all hoping to be crowned king or queen of the Hellswan kingdom, but I'd been too preoccupied to count exactly how many.

"Twenty men and women, including me," he replied, "and we all start on zero points, except Ash, who has twenty points from the first trial."

"And what about the first trial—have they found out who tampered with the disk?"

"No," he replied curtly, "announcing a new king is the priority."

That seemed short-sighted of the ministers. If the trials continued to be jeopardized, then they'd be left with a bunch of dead wannabe kings.

"When does the next trial start?" I asked, beginning to feel frustrated by the lack of forthcoming information.

"Tomorrow."

Tomorrow?

"They want to get going as soon as possible," he continued, apparently unaware of how anxious I'd suddenly become. "The next trial will begin tomorrow afternoon. And before you ask"—he furrowed his brows—"no, I have no idea what it will entail."

Hazel

At around noon the next day, Tejus and I followed the procession of ministers and the red-robed 'watchers' who had attempted to referee the last trial. They led us through the castle courtyard and through another wide arch in the defensive walls that surrounded the grounds. We passed a heavily armed gatehouse with a raised portcullis. A wide bridge over the moat lay ahead, and then greenish-brown meadows dipped and rose down to a large lake.

The crowd had already gathered there, waving banners and chanting for the champions. As we reached the lake, I could see that wooden seating had been set up to surround the water, with the royal box at the far end filled with the most finely dressed sentries. I expected to see a black flag covering the box—or something to indicate the Emperor's passing—but I saw nothing.

"You should stay behind me at all times," Tejus instructed quietly, "and don't get lost in the crowd."

I nodded, distracted with looking for Ruby and Ash. I couldn't see them anywhere, but a roar of approval from the crowd soon alerted me to their presence.

Ash stepped out into the clearing with Ruby at his side. They waved to their fans, those seated in the lower tiers of the benches— servants and castle staff—before the ministers hustled them both over to the rest of the waiting champions.

They were too far ahead for me to see Ruby properly, but every so often I got a glimpse of her blonde hair and calm expression, her blue eyes focused on Ash.

"Is she a friend of yours?"

A voice behind me made me turn around, and I looked up into the smiling eyes of a very handsome sentry with short, cropped blond hair and grayish eyes. Weirdly, he reminded me a bit of Wes.

"Uh, yes, she's a friend. Why?" I asked, confused.

"No reason," he replied. "I've been racking my brain the last few minutes for a way to start a conversation with you, and that seemed as good an opener as any."

He winked at me, and stupidly, I found myself blushing.

"You're competing in the trials," I commented—he was dressed in robes, and laden down with weapons.

"I am… I'm the son of one of the ministers. You'll see my mother up there." He pointed to a ferocious-looking, tight lipped minister wearing a thunderous expression. "She's proud of me—though you wouldn't know it to look at her." He smirked.

Something nudged him and he looked down. "Oh, this is my human helper, *Chris*." A young boy had appeared around his robe, and looked up at me nervously. "Chris, say hello," he prompted the boy, and gently pushed him forward.

"Hello," Chris whispered, and then disappeared back behind the sentry.

"My mother took him," he explained on seeing my disturbed expression, "but I plan to send him back home as soon as the Hellswan borders are re-opened—"

"Hazel!" Tejus called to me before I could respond. He was standing five feet away, seemingly irritated that I wasn't right behind him.

"I'm Nikolay, by the way," the handsome sentry said as

I turned to leave. "Good luck in the trial, *Hazel*."

I waved awkwardly goodbye, slightly relieved to be getting back to the relative comfort of Tejus's presence. Tejus glowered at me as I approached, and I shrugged innocently. I didn't understand what his problem was – was he now going to try and forbid me from talking to the other champions? I suspected that if he thought he could get away with it, he would.

Up ahead, one of the ministers cleared his throat and motioned for silence. I recognized him as the same one who had announced the first trial.

"Sentries, welcome," he announced. "Today we commence the second trial for kingship—a trial that will test the mettle of our esteemed and hopeful champions. Our second trial relies on unity—unity because we know that a king is only as good and strong as his people, and the right leader of Hellswan will know both when to lead and when to follow." There was a round of applause, and more cheering from the servants for Ash.

"The rules!" the minister announced. "The winners of this trial will be the two champions who reach the golden chains of solidarity first." He gestured to two gold chains at the far end of the lake, hanging suspended in the air and glinting in the sunlight. "They will each be awarded twenty points, with those who follow being awarded only ten. Those who fail to reach the other side of the lake will be instantly disqualified. So too will anyone caught using mind manipulation on living creatures... you will have a chance to demonstrate those skills in the trials to come. And finally, remember that waters hold hidden depths, and creatures that should never be seen... Let the trials begin!"

With a theatrical flourish, the minister ended his speech, standing back from the water's edge.

Tejus motioned for me to stay put, and moved forward with the rest of the champions. I looked at the still, calm waters of the lake. If I didn't know any better, I would have thought that this trial was a piece of cake, but I dreaded to think what was waiting beneath the placidly rippling surface. Ruby came to stand by my side, and together we watched the champions approach the water.

They held their weapons aloft and moved at a measured pace, but I could tell the suspense was getting to them. A few at the front clearly wanted to dive straight into the lake and swim across to grab the chains, but they were hesitant.

An impatient cry sounded from within the crowd, and eventually one of the champions took a running leap into the water, sword at the ready. He was followed by two more, and they each disappeared below the surface.

"ARGH!" They popped up, one by one, screaming bloodcurdling cries as large white and blue-gray tentacles, almost translucent in their milky hue, wrapped around their faces and limbs. As they thrashed about in the water, I could see the spidery veins of the creatures starting to turn red—they were sucking blood from their victims.

The crowd cried out in horror, and the red-robed watchers dragged the victims out, removing the creatures by throwing what looked like buckets of salt over them till they withered up and fell to the ground. Their victims audibly groaned, and I heaved a sigh of relief that they were still alive.

The rest of the sentries looked about them in confusion. I searched for the familiar figure of Tejus, and found him away from all the commotion, standing further along the bank, looking out over the water.

As I watched, Ash approached him and leaned forward, whispering something in his ear and gesturing over at the chains. Tejus gave him a brief nod, and they both started to make their way back to where Ruby and I stood waiting.

"Ash has come up with a plan," Tejus announced in a hushed voice, "I need you now, Hazel. Are you ready?" His gaze was penetrating and I gulped. I was ready. Without thinking I dug my hand into the pocket of my robe, and felt for the cool, reassuring presence of the sword stone.

Tejus glanced at Ash, who was briefing Ruby in a far warmer manner. Ash nodded back at him and they both made their way, side by side, to the water's edge. Ruby and I followed.

I felt the feathery strokes brush against the insides of my temples, a sign that Tejus was beginning to siphon off my energy. I felt the slight tug as the connection was made, and the dull throbbing as he borrowed from me—slowly sucking away at my mind.

I clasped the stone when it started to feel uncomfortable, and felt a release of exhilaration traveling through my body. At the same time, I could sort of *feel* Tejus expending energy and power, but when I looked over at them, he and Ash appeared to be doing nothing— just standing motionless by the lake.

Looking over at Ruby, I searched her expression to see if she was any the wiser, but she looked just as baffled as I felt.

As I watched, Tejus took a step forward. I was about to cry out, to run after him and haul him back, but his foot didn't come into contact with the water—it hovered a few inches above it. He took another step, and Ash did the same.

Oh, smart.

I suddenly realized what they had done. Together they had created a barrier over the water—the same type of invisible barrier the ministers had put up around Hellswan that was holding us back from leaving the kingdom, or anyone getting in. I hadn't realized that all sentries had that ability.

Ruby exhaled a sigh of relief next to me, but looked as stunned as I did at what Tejus and Ash could do.

"Did you know that was even possible for anyone other than the ministers?" she asked me.

I shook my head, speechless.

The crowd soon realized what the two champions were doing. They roared and cheered Ash's name, all rising from their benches in honor.

I had just let myself relax, seeing the pair of them start to run across the water – a mere few yards from the glinting chains, when my blood ran cold.

A single tentacle had risen out of the water. It's translucent skin wavered about in the air, running alongside what I presumed was the barrier that Ash and Tejus had created.

"Tejus, look out!" I screamed, once, but it was too late.

The tentacle came hurtling toward him, long enough to reach over the barrier, and swifter than I could have imagined. Tejus turned, just in time to see the pulsing monstrosity looming over him. I saw him reach for his sword, but as soon as he grasped it, the tentacle knocked it out of his hand and it skidded across the smooth surface of the barrier. Tejus suddenly jerked upward, batting the tentacle back with something in his hand. The blue-grey limb thrashed wildly, almost knocking Ash into the water, who'd come to stand beside Tejus, sword at the ready. Blue-black liquid squirted from a wound in the tentacle, showering Tejus and Ash. Tejus held a dagger aloft, ready for the next strike.

By this time, using the distraction to their advantage, the other champions began to create their own barriers. Two sentries, who were running across the lake, skidded on the surface of their barrier. One of the sentries screamed out in fear, grabbing wildly at air as he tried to avoid the lake below. The tentacle that had been so intent on bringing Tejus down, now swiftly ducked back down into the water, reappearing seconds later to grab the falling sentry.

Tejus and Ash quickly regained their bearings and started to run toward the chains. I felt dizzy with relief, and as they landed on the other side of the lake – each grasping their reward and holding it aloft, I took a huge gulp of air, only just realizing that I'd not taken a breath since the tentacle had emerged from the lake.

They had won the trial.

Tejus held his chain out to the ministers, Ash held his out to the adoring crowds. Ruby clutched my hand tightly, and we each beamed at each other with a mixture of relief and joy.

One down!

Amidst the cheers were more screams of pain and horror as some of the other sentries' barriers broke. A couple had tried to do it on their own, but were not strong enough to hold the barrier in place as they crossed it. They had fallen into the water, the putrid tentacles rising out of the water once again to claim their victims, as the fallen sentries screamed in agony.

I counted six champions who would now be out of the running.

"Bravo!" cried the minister who had announced the trial, stepping forward once again to congratulate the heroes.

"Tejus and Ashbik win the second round," he declared, "awarding them twenty points each, which leaves Ashbik still in the lead with forty points in total." Another ferocious roar went up from the crowd. "Ten points are awarded to each champion who made it across the lake." Smaller pockets of applause erupted around the crowd. "Those who didn't, I'm afraid to say, are disqualified."

I did a quick mental calculation. That left fourteen champions left in the running—including Ash and Tejus. As the champions made their way along the far end of the lake to rejoin the crowd, I couldn't help but notice the golden hair of Nikolay—he had made it too.

Ministers and watchers attended to the groaning sentries lying on the banks of the lake. They might not have been in any mortal danger, but it struck me just how brutal these trials were. It seemed the modus operandi in Nevertide was sink or swim, literally, and I felt a slight unfurling of dread at what was still to come.

RUBY

"I realized this afternoon that I haven't shown you the nicer parts of the castle," Ash said, leading me off through another narrow corridor. He'd been removed from kitchen duty as soon as the competition had started, and a few hours after we'd returned to the castle, he'd appeared at the door of my room, excitement buzzing beneath the surface of his usual composure.

"Where are we going?" I asked, taken aback that there were parts of the castle that Ash considered 'nice'—at times I felt he loathed Hellswan Kingdom more than we did, and it had been his home all his life.

"You'll see," he answered vaguely, taking my hand in

his to drag me onward. It was lukewarm and calloused, and at its familiar touch I recalled the moment that the same hand had pulled me from the cellar that Jenus had held us captive in—the reassuring strength of it as comforting now as it had been then.

We came to a small doorway right at the back of one of the castle turrets, an area that I hadn't previously seen. Ash retrieved a wizened key, and turned the lock. The door creaked open as if it hadn't done so for centuries, but when he revealed what lay behind it I gasped involuntarily.

"Beautiful, isn't it?' Ash asked, his voice full of reverence. I was too stunned to speak.

The door had opened onto a small, walled garden. Small stepping stones weaved in and out of lush greenery and bright flowers, roses climbed up the walls and produced large bouquets of sweet-smelling blooms. Every available surface was completely covered in a multitude of bright colors or dark, thick-leaved shrubbery.

"Who looks after this? It's *incredible*," I whispered.

Ash smiled. "I actually don't know. Hellswan has gardeners, but none of them would be up to this... Jenney and I found it years ago, but we never mentioned it to any of the other kitchen staff. Seemed like it was a bit too nice to share." He shrugged. "But I thought we could have a picnic here or something—celebrate our win."

A picnic in this picturesque place sounded a bit too romantic for comfort. A large part of me wanted to say yes, and I didn't want to read too much into it... I knew Ash and I made a good team, and a bond was steadily growing between us—partly due to our increasingly successful mind melds, and partly due to our shared goal in winning the trials. But I didn't know if it was wise to get involved in *that* way.

There was a lot at stake.

"Uh, okay," I replied trying to sound light, but my hesitation had given me away.

Ash's expression was unreadable, but when he answered me his tone was gentle. "Why don't we just have a walk and we can go back to eat with the others? Jenney will only moan if she has to cart our dinner out here anyway."

"Okay," I said again, feeling reassured that I hadn't hurt his feelings.

Ash carried on down the pathway, navigating his brawn gracefully over the stones. The garden was a lot larger than I'd first assumed and soon we were so deep in its thicket that I couldn't see the surrounding walls.

"What made you think of the barriers?" I asked after a while. "That was quite impressive – I didn't even know you could do that. I don't think that Tejus would have arrived at the same conclusion without you."

"All sentries have the ability – but it takes more than one of us, and if I'm honest, it's not really my best skill." Then Ash chuckled. "There was something about one of the other champions sitting on the bank, looking completely offended and disoriented after the water beasts got him, that reminded me of *you*—when I saw you on your ass in the dirt after the Nevertide barrier bounced you back."

"Glad I was such an inspiration."

"Let's just say that image won't leave me for a while." He smirked at me.

My cheeks heated.

"I guess it's just a shame that Hellswan got points too," Ash continued gloomily, "but I didn't know any of the others well enough to know if their mind control was up to it."

"You did the right thing," I said, "you're still twenty points ahead."

Ash cast a watchful eye across the garden. "Yeah, I know. But I didn't want him gaining any. I think the bastard's got guards watching me." He lowered his voice. "I'm worried he knows about the Emperor."

My stomach lurched queasily. Ash had poisoned the Emperor—just enough to knock him out for a few days and distract Jenus while Ash rescued us from the cellar, but somehow it had gone wrong and the Emperor had died. If Tejus had suspicions that Ash was involved, then it wouldn't take much for a conviction—a royal's word against a servant's.

"What makes you think that?" I asked quietly.

"Nothing concrete." He hesitated. "I just get a *feeling*—like I'm being watched. I'll be walking down a hallway or alone in the kitchen and I can feel eyes on me." He shivered. "It's making me jumpy."

I felt a bit relieved at his account. "Sounds like it might just be your imagination. Or he's doing it to distract you from the trials. No one's said anything yet, have they?"

"No." He scratched his head. "Maybe you're right. Maybe I'm just imagining it—guilty conscience and all that."

I nodded. That sounded more likely. I couldn't imagine that Tejus would wait around—if he had evidence he'd act fast, and try his best to get Ash kicked out of the trials and disqualified. I didn't believe that Tejus truly cared for his father—what I believed he cared about was his rise to power.

"You just need to focus on the trials, Ash," I reminded him. "Forget the Emperor. Hellswan—and all of Nevertide—needs you."

He nodded slowly, the tension draining from him.

"Is there anything I can do?" I added. "To help?"

He was about to shake his head in a 'no', but then he stopped.

"You know, perhaps if we mind-meld again... that might help. I seem to feel stronger after we do that—as long as you're up for it?" he added, looking at me with an open expression.

"Okay."

A few yards ahead of us was what looked like a small sycamore tree, surrounded by a grassy verge. I gestured over to it, and Ash led the way. We sat beneath the tree, each on either side of its trunk, our backs against the smooth bark.

I relaxed, and concentrated on 'throwing' my mind out to Ash. I felt our energy meet, winding around the trunk of the tree, and a blissful calm settling over me. Against the black of my closed eyes, I could see bright colors forming—brilliant turquoises, blues and ambers, all dancing and flitting between each other and intertwining to create new, vivid colors. It was like having our own private fireworks show, and I passed the thought along to Ash. I felt him chuckle in response, and a very small, quick image flashed up in my conscience. It was of two people who looked very much like Ash and me sitting in the garden eating a picnic as the sun set. In an instant the picture was gone, and replaced by more dancing colors.

Oh.

I felt him try to leave the mind meld, pulling away from me. I tried to resist and hold on to the energy, wanting to show him I was sorry that I'd said no to a picnic, but he didn't let me. Then the connection broke abruptly.

Ash stood up, and came over, offering me his hand.

"Come on, shortie... I'm just hungry."

"Okay," I muttered, annoyed that our connection had come to an end so quickly.

As we walked back down the path we'd entered, the garden stopped feeling so lovely and the big leaves and thickets that tugged at my clothes became irritating—I was glad when we finally saw the door to the castle up ahead.

I couldn't help but think that we *should* have continued the mind meld. It did make our connection stronger, and made it easier for Ash to siphon off me, which was important for the trials.

I guessed this was exactly why I didn't want anything

more getting in the way—one request for a picnic from Ash and already we were in awkward territory, trials momentarily forgotten.

It came as a firm warning to me that we had to keep things businesslike between us… as much as we actually could.

BENEDICT

Julian and I were playing Snap when the guards entered. I was glad they came when they did, because Julian had won every single hand and was starting to boast about his quick reflexes. I just didn't have the energy. Every movement I made felt like I was wading through mud, and my thought process was so slow I could barely string a sentence together. I would have found it frustrating, but I found I didn't even really care that much—all I wanted to do was go to sleep.

"Ministers here to see you," announced the guard.

"Ruby isn't here. Neither's Hazel," Julian called back to him, barely looking up from the table.

"Ministers are here to see *you two*," he barked back.

We rose to our feet, both wondering what the ministers could possibly want with us. They swept into the room, looking like a group of ghosts on account of their black robes and pale, menacing faces.

"Julian and Benedict?" one of the ministers enquired. He was a tall, emaciated-looking man, wearing large, round glasses that made his eyes appear too large for his face.

"What do you want?" Julian asked.

I nudged Julian—his tone was too abrupt, and I felt that we should at least pretend to be polite to the ministers. I didn't fancy being sent back down to the servants' quarters to sleep on Ash's lumpy bed again.

"We have a small issue we were hoping the two of you could assist us with," the man replied, ignoring Julian's lack of manners.

"What is it?" I mumbled.

A woman stepped forward, and I recognized her as the thin-lipped woman I'd overheard whispering outside the Emperor's room.

"As you know, many of the sentries are using humans to increase their mental agility—"

"*Kidnapped* humans," retorted Julian.

"As I was saying," the woman continued, "the kidnapped humans the champions have been using have nowhere to go now that their champions have been knocked out of the running, and we can't release them until the Hellswan barriers are down—which we absolutely *cannot* do until we have a new ruler in place." She eyed Julian, daring him to protest. When he didn't, she continued, "So, we are at a loss as to what to do with them, and we thought that perhaps it might be easiest if they were to stay with *you*."

"It appears you have the space," added the man dryly, looking about the huge—and empty—living quarters.

"But not the resources," Julian said. "You'd need to give us clothes and food for them."

The woman eyed him shrewdly. "The kitchen will be able to assist you, and I will ensure that clean clothing is provided."

She didn't look too happy about her new responsibility, but I was glad that Julian was taking advantage of us having the upper hand. Plus, they were the ones that had put up the barriers in the first place…this was their doing.

"I shall bring them along to you shortly. There will be six coming today—more, no doubt, tomorrow." She turned back toward the door, the other ministers following her lead. Clearly the conversation was over.

Six?

It seemed like a lot, even for the amount of space we had. I didn't really know where they would all sleep, especially if more came.

"We need Jenney," Julian said.

I nodded. I didn't know how to begin looking after a bunch of displaced kids—I could only imagine the state that some of them might be in. We were lucky, I supposed, that we'd been kidnapped as a group. Most of these children would have been taken alone, and left to navigate the terrifying realities of mind-sucking sentries and Nevertide on their own.

Ruby and Hazel would know what to do, but they were off with their champions… doing God knew what.

About an hour after they'd left us, the ministers returned with the six humans.

"Here they are," trilled the woman, shoving them into the room. "I've told the kitchen staff. They're your responsibility now."

Her eyes gleamed. Clearly she was glad to be rid of them. She slammed the door shut behind her, and I imagined it would be the last time she'd set foot in here for the foreseeable future.

Julian and I stared at the assortment of bedraggled humans standing in the middle of the living quarters. I counted six, as she'd promised.

"Who are you?" one grubby-looking girl demanded. She had bright blue eyes and matted hair which was probably once red, and wore nothing more than sackcloth. Even so, with her hands on her hips and her chin jutting out, she looked like a potential pain in the backside.

"I'm Benedict, this is Julian," I replied. "We've been put in charge of all the humans till we can all get back home. You're staying here with us."

"*Here?*" she asked, looking about the room with boggling eyes. "But this isn't where the humans stay!"

"It is in Hellswan," corrected Julian. "Shortly we'll assign you each a bed, and food will be brought up. Most of you need a bath." He surveyed them all, some cleaner-looking than the others, but still in need of some fresh clothes and a hairbrush. "I'll get someone to help with that. Just take a seat here"—he gestured to the sofas in the middle of the room—"and wait with Benedict."

Huh?

I stared at him. I wasn't comfortable being left alone with them—the youngest looked about five, what if he started crying?

"I'm going to find Jenney," he said to me. "You'll be fine!"

With that, he marched out of the door.

"Uh… okay." I hesitated, trying to come up with something we could do till Julian returned. "Why don't you all tell me your names, and a bit about where you came from originally?"

"I'll start," announced the blue-eyed girl. "I'm Yelena, I'm twelve, and I was taken from Rome in Italy, when I was on holiday with my parents. They tried to make me stand in a line to see some stupid old monument and so I ran off for ice-cream, but was kidnapped and brought here instead."

For such a traumatic experience, she seemed quite upbeat about it. Perhaps her sentry hadn't been that bad, though she certainly didn't look well-kept.

The names and the stories continued. The youngest one, the boy I'd thought was five—who was actually seven, but so malnourished that I couldn't tell—hung on to Yelena's arm the entire time and sniffled. I wanted Ruby or Hazel to be here—they would have known what to do with him. All I could manage was what I hoped was a reassuring smile in his direction.

"So how come you're living in a place like this?" Yelena

asked. "How come *you're* being treated like royalty?"

I frowned at her. She was already starting to irritate me with her accusatory tone and I made a mental note to ask Julian to put her bed *miles* from mine.

"Our friend and my sister, Hazel, are helping Ash and Tejus—the prince of Hellswan. That's why we're getting special treatment. They're the two likeliest champions—everyone's saying so," I replied huffily.

"The kitchen boy's the likeliest champion?" Yelena scoffed. "I don't *think* so."

"Oh, yeah, who was your champion? They obviously didn't do very well," I retorted.

She rolled her eyes at me and flung herself backward on the sofa.

Girls!

Thankfully Jenney and Julian re-entered the room, and I left the kids sitting on the sofa. They were odd. Most of them just kept looking around, as if something was about to jump out at them.

"How are they doing?" Julian asked in a faux whisper that could definitely be heard across the room.

"Fine," I replied shortly.

"All right, kids!" Jenney shouted, ignoring both Julian and me. "Who wants a bath?"

If their parents could have seen the enthusiastic response that resulted, they would have been proud. They all scrambled up from the sofa and rushed to Jenney as though she were holding a tray of chocolate doughnuts.

Jenney led them out of the room, saying that she was taking them to a larger bathing area in the main quarters of the castle. Other servants emerged with an assortment of bedding, and Julian and I set about rearranging it so that we had enough space for the six to sleep, and more when it was needed.

"We should have a girls' area and a boys' area," I said to Julian, thinking of Yelena.

"Okay," he agreed.

Other than the room that Julian and I were sharing, and Ruby's room, there were five other rooms—some with beds, some just containing shelves and large chests or broken furniture. We cleared them as best we could and made up makeshift beds.

"That should be enough for now," Julian said. "We can make more if we need to. But they'll have to start sleeping out in the living room."

"Well"—I shrugged—"at least we know the sofas are comfy."

"This is going to be fun, isn't it?" he muttered.

I thought of the downtrodden seven-year-old with the sniffles, and chatterbox Yelena.

Yeah, you can say that again.

Hazel

Two carriages had come this morning to take Tejus and me, and Ruby and Ash, to the third trial. They had been driven by guards, and were pulled along by the strangest half-horse, half-bull creatures. The drive had been about an hour, and when we disembarked, we were surrounded by green rolling hills and open meadows. The walk down to the ravine would have been a pleasant one, were it not for the lurching anticipation I was experiencing. Tejus, on the other hand, appeared completely calm in the face of the upcoming trial. It was kind of irritating.

I looked up at the dusty, dry banks from the bottom of the ravine. They were easily seven or eight meters high, with thin edges creating a causeway on which to climb to the top. I took a step forward, and heard a gloopy sound as my boot got caught in the thick silt that had been left behind by the river.

Tejus pointed to the dark black holes that were dotted along the bank walls. "See these? They're the caves of Helic—legend has it they have mythical properties, and used to be home to water sprites."

They certainly looked dark and foreboding, and I had a sickening feeling that they would house today's trial.

"Are you stuck?" asked a familiar voice from behind me.

"Oh. Thanks," I murmured, as Nikolay leant down to help me remove my boot from the mud.

"How are you feeling?" he asked, smiling up at me from his crouched position on the ground. Even surrounded by a smelly and muddy ravine, his good looks made my heart hammer more energetically than it should.

"I'm fine," I muttered.

"Oh, come on, everyone knows these trials are harder on the humans than they are on the sentries."

"Hazel!" Tejus called, making me jump.

"What?" I replied irritably, wishing he'd stop sounding so commanding all the time—it was starting to wear *very* thin.

"We need to get up there. What are you doing?" He glared at Nikolay, then back at me. Nikolay bowed his head respectfully.

"Good luck to both of you," Nikolay uttered, smiling at me alone. Then he walked back the way he'd come.

"Will you focus for one minute?" Tejus said.

"My foot got stuck and Nikolay was kind enough to help me!" I hissed.

"Well, if we fail, you'll have all the time in the world for conversations because you'll be stuck in Nevertide forever."

I clenched my fists. "Let's go then!" I flounced off in the direction of the causeway, where I could see other champions and their humans all ascending one by one.

The crowd had also started to arrive. I turned my head to face the opposite wall of the bank, and could see them all sitting and standing at the edge, with a good view into the caves.

I could hear Tejus walking behind me, and we rapidly made our way up to the rows of caves. Red-robed watchers were directing the sentries to the opening of individual caves, and Tejus and I were assigned the one furthest away. As we walked along the causeway, I saw Ash and Ruby standing outside one of the caves, three before ours. I waved at Ruby and she smiled back at me, but her eyes reflected her unease.

We approached our assigned spot, and I noticed a small, freshly dug hole at its entrance. I looked back. At every cave entrance I could see the same small hole.

"What do you think those are?" I asked Tejus, my previous irritation with him forgotten.

"I don't know," he replied, observing the hole. He shrugged. "Maybe we put something in it that we get from the cave. They go back for miles."

I peered inside. It was almost pitch black, but the dark didn't frighten me. It was what might lie in its shadows that I was concerned with. I very much doubted that this was going to be a family-fun treasure hunt.

Tejus's gaze was now directed at the crowds on the other side of the bank.

"They really love him, don't they?" he mused softly.

I saw what he meant. Team Ash was out in full force today. New flags had been created, not of the insignia of the kingdom, but from the same brown material of the servants' uniforms that they wore in Hellswan castle. They chanted his name, and their echoes were amplified throughout the ravine.

"They love the *idea* of him," I concluded. "He hasn't

ruled them, and so they can project their ideas and dreams onto him."

Tejus looked at me with his eyebrows raised.

"You are sometimes surprising," he remarked.

Before I could ask what he meant exactly, the crowd started to hush, and the minister of ceremonies stepped out from the far end of the causeway.

"Welcome," he announced grandly, "to the third, and possibly the most important event of the kingship trials."

The crowd roared with approval, and I glanced at Tejus. His expression seemed set in stone, no facial tic giving away what he might be feeling on the inside.

"Today we will test our champions' honesty, that they may come to understand their own truth, in order to see honor and honesty in others. The truth will set us free, and only unchained and proud can we hope to rule our people."

Proud was right.

"Watchers will be delivering a liquid for each champion to consume," he continued, and I watched as the red robes filed down the causeway, handing each champion a bottle of amber-colored liquid.

"This liquid is taken from the flower *honestas*, native to our land. Many of you will know it to have hallucinatory properties, but do not be alarmed, the visions you will see will be the product of your imagination alone. You will face your innermost self in the caves—and *that* is what you will battle today.

"The winner will be the first to emerge from the caves with the golden seed and plant it into the earth." He gestured to the row of small holes that lay at each cave. "Those who come out of the cave without the seeds forfeit the trials."

A low horn sounded, and Tejus lifted the glass vial he'd been handed into the air. It glowed briefly in the sun, and then he swallowed the contents without leaving a drop.

"Stay behind me, but mind to keep out of my way. I don't know what will happen, or what I will become in those caves. I know this liquid well. Its effects are all-consuming and absolute."

With his warning ringing in my ears, I followed him into the darkness of the cave.

In the absolute pitch black, I felt his mind reach out for mine. When our energy met, I felt his grasp strongly—it wasn't the light feathery touches that I usually experienced, but more of an intense probing sensation that caused my temples to throb. I could feel his trepidation and anxiety filtering down our bond. I realized that the grasp was so tight because he was *afraid*.

In a strange way, I understood instantly that the one thing that Tejus would be afraid of was himself.

I clutched at the stone within my robes, and instantly the throbbing in my head died down. In the next moment, I was aware that I could see what Tejus was seeing—my viewpoint changing to being ahead in the cave—and I could no longer see the dark shadow of Tejus standing before me.

I fought the strangeness of the feeling, and settled into accepting that I seemed to no longer be in my own mind.

Tejus spun around, looking toward the light of the cave... but my body was gone. I should have been standing behind him, and I could feel that I still was, but Tejus couldn't see me.

Waves of isolation and panic washed over him, and he called out into the darkness, "Hazel! Where are you?"

I tried to send my presence over the bond, as if I was knocking on the door to his mind, but either I wasn't strong enough to do it, or the hallucination was set so deep that he couldn't feel or hear me.

"I'm here!" I called out, but his mind didn't register my presence. It was like I'd completely disappeared.

Instead, visions started to form in front of him. They

were just shapes and wisps of gray at first, but soon they started to take on solid outlines, and I could make out the Hellswan castle, dark and looming with the moonlight behind it. Tejus focused on one of the towers, the furthest on the right, and a small, puppet-like figure flew out from one of the windows and down onto the ground below.

It was a sickening image. Even though I couldn't discern any facial features of the figure, the flying, helpless body and the stillness after it smacked into the ground was horrifying.

I could practically taste Tejus's fear and despair as he watched the image. No sooner had the scene played out than it started up again on a macabre loop—the figure appearing at the window, and its fall to the ground below.

His brother.

I finally realized what we were seeing. It was his brother, Danto, the one who had supposedly committed suicide the night before the trial the emperor had prepared for his sons—where each one of them fought their way through his despicable labyrinth to win the sword of Hellswan and be put forward as the champion.

Tejus closed his eyes as if he could block out the image, and I could feel the effort he was expelling trying to remove it from his mind.

I clutched the stone harder, wanting the image to be gone as badly as he did.

Eventually it started to fade.

The gray wisps and shadows returned, and started to form again. This time we were inside the castle. Burning torches lined the walls, and the vulture heads set in gold gleamed in light.

A young boy appeared in the corridor, smiling as he walked toward us. He was very pale, with dark hair, his robes trailing along on the stone floor behind him. I wouldn't have recognized him in a million years had it not been for the fact that I'd seen him in another vision of Tejus's—an old memory that he'd shared with me a few nights ago.

The boy was Jenus, his banished brother.

The boy opened his mouth, trying to say something, but no sound was coming out. He started to look cross, repeating himself and clenching his fists.

I held the stone more tightly, trying to focus on the movement of the boy's lips, willing for sound to come out. A high-pitched whine echoed around the cave, as if someone was turning a dial on an old radio and getting nothing but white noise. It settled down, and the boy's voice could be heard faintly, as if it was coming from the very depths of the cave.

"It's not fair, Tejus!" the cry came. "You spend all your time with the others… you never want to play with me… what's so wrong with *me*?"

The childish plea was harrowing—not because of what was being said, I was pretty positive Benedict had moaned at me in a similar way before, but it was the fact that it was so well remembered, so full of resentment and anguish.

The image vanished.

Gray wisps re-formed, swirling ferociously this time, as Tejus's mood became blacker and more hopeless. Another image stood before us. This time it was Jenus as an adult, his large frame slightly bent and his greasy long hair hanging loose over his black robe. His back was to Tejus, and he was walking away, following the trail to black nothingness in the pits of the cave.

Tejus called out his name, but Jenus didn't turn around.

Tejus fell to his knees, and the bond we shared was awash with a terrible sense of loss and loneliness.

"Forgive me," Tejus said. "I have failed you, brother, and I am alone. I am lost, that is my *truth*," he spat out the words, "there is no one left who gives a damn."

I wanted to shout out and tell him that he was wrong— it was just the hallucination playing tricks on him—but before I could say a word, a shaft of light appeared above us in the rock, and something rolled down, landing with a soft thud in Tejus's open hands.

The golden seed.

It gleamed in the dull light, and suddenly I was pushed out of Tejus's mind and was back in my own, standing behind him as I had been the entire time.

Tejus jumped to his feet, his face slowly lighting up with victory. The feelings that he had been drowning in a moment ago ceased to exist, and he rushed out from the cave and into the bright light, dragging me by the arm.

RUBY

Ash drank down the liquid, grimacing as he did so. I reached for his hand, and he clasped it in his. We entered the cave together, my heart thudding in my chest as we entered the gloom.

I didn't know what to expect, and I didn't think Ash did either, so we just stood in the darkness, side by side, waiting for something to happen.

Soon enough, Ash started to shake, the fingers that encased mine starting to tremble. I could just make out his expression, and soon wished I couldn't. His eyes were open wide at some inexplicable horror that only he could see.

I closed my eyes, trying to get a grasp on his energy,

reaching out with my mind so that he could take some comfort from it and quell whatever fear he was facing. I sent calming and tranquil energy through our bond when I felt it form, but he resisted it.

"No…" he whispered. "I think this is something that I need to face on my own."

He let go of my hand and ran his hands through his hair as if he wanted to tear it all out. His eyes grew wider still, and I could see perspiration forming above his brow.

"What can you see?" I asked, hating that he was enduring this alone.

"It's…it's the Emperor," he stuttered, "everywhere… his body is everywhere. The dead Emperor."

I felt sick.

Is this some kind of joke?

But no, it was just a hallucination. A figment of Ash's imagination.

"It's not real," I replied, trying to soothe him, "it's just tricks in your mind."

"But it *is* the truth," he whispered back in a tremoring voice. "I have done this…"

"No, Ash! This is the liquid—you need to focus on the task—can you see the seed?" I cried, imploring him to stay in reality and keep his mind on the trial.

"I can see it." He blanched. "But it's all the way over there."

He pointed to the other end of the cave, and I squinted. Sure enough, a dull glint appeared in the gloom. I stepped forward—if Ash was unable to reach it for whatever reason, there was nothing stopping me from doing so.

"Stop!" he said. "I need to do this. This is my responsibility."

"Can you get to it?" I asked, feeling a bit stupid. The path to the stone was completely clear to me.

"Yes, I just need to stand on the… the bodies—I need to stand on the Emperor's body to reach it." He gulped.

He took a step. He looked like he was going to be sick, but he kept his eyes ahead, fixed on the stone.

"You can do it, Ash," I whispered. I felt completely useless—but if he wouldn't let me use our bond to send him peaceful thoughts, then there was little I could do but stand and watch.

"This is my truth," he suddenly announced to the room in a low, solemn voice, "I am ruthless. I will stop at *nothing* to achieve my goals."

He took another step toward the seed, and then visibly relaxed. Whatever had been haunting him had gone.

Ash grabbed the seed, and turned around to face me.

He held it aloft, panting slightly from the exertion of the last few minutes, and then ran toward the opening of the cave. I followed him.

We raced toward the hole in the earth, cheers erupting from the crowd as Ash emerged from the cave. He bent down to place the seed in the earth. Out of the corner of my eye, I could see Tejus further down the causeway, doing exactly the same thing.

Was it a tie?

The crowd fell silent as it collectively held its breath.

"Well, congratulations!" cried the minister, making his way along the causeway to the two caves. "It seems we have a close call, but I believe Tejus was, in fact, first out of the cave."

A red-robed watcher whispered in the minister's ear, and his beaming smile faltered momentarily before he regained his composure.

"Yes, I think that Tejus was in fact—"

"One moment, please!" a voice called out from the royal box in the center of the crowd, and I recognized the blue robes and black hair of the same woman who had spoken out for Ash in the disk trial.

"I believe that you, esteemed minister, are wrong. It was Ash who planted the seed first—Ash who was first out of the cave. It is *he* who is, in fact, the winner of this trial."

Cheering erupted once again from the crowd, and the minister's face became contorted by fury.

"I am sorry, Queen Trina, but our watchers here almost unanimously agree that it was Prince Tejus who emerged from the cave first."

The watcher opened his mouth to speak, but the minister quickly silenced him with a raised hand.

"With all due respect, your highness, you couldn't have possibly seen the details correctly from your position," he continued. "You are too far—whereas our watchers are trained for this kind of thing, and were closer to the action."

"Minister," the queen sharply reprimanded him, "have you forgotten who has the best gift of True Sight in all the kingdoms? My skills are unequaled, and I tell you Ash was first out!"

I supposed by 'true sight' she meant what Ash could do—the ability of some sentries to see far ahead in the distance, and through whatever might stand in their way. If that was true, maybe Ash *had* won the trial.

The red-robed watcher, sick of being ignored, burst out, "I agree. Queen Trina is correct—it was Ashbik who was the first champion out of the cave!"

No sooner had the words left his mouth than another champion came tearing out, his hands clutched over his eyes. "No, no, no!" he cried, over and over again. He dropped to the floor and cowered there, crouched in a fetal position, his body tremoring.

The crowd gasped, and the crying sentry was followed by another, then another. Some emerged victorious, white-faced and drenched in sweat, but more often they didn't and collapsed on the ground, or ran off into the meadows as if the devil himself was chasing them.

The crowd started murmuring, and soon a slow chant erupted from a small pocket of sentries, and spread out till the entire crowd were crying Ash's name.

"Order!" commanded the minister. "It seems I stand corrected. Ashbik is the winner of this trial, gaining twenty points. Tejus gains ten points, as do all the others who emerged with the golden seed."

The muttering of the ministers standing by the royal box grew. One look at their faces and I could tell that they, like the minister of ceremony, were vastly displeased with the outcome. It wasn't the same with the crowd. They applauded loudly, and Ash took a bow, grabbing my hand again, as we smiled and waved at our cheerleaders.

I glanced over at Tejus and Hazel. She looked downcast,

her eyes fixed on the floor, and I wanted to walk over and talk to her—and would have were it not for the looming presence of Tejus by her side. He stood unmoving and expressionless as if the outcome of the trial didn't affect him in anyway.

I looked back at Ash, still waving at the crowds with a huge grin on his face, and I felt suddenly afraid for him.

What might Tejus be capable of if he didn't win the trials?

Hazel

Tejus sat on the sofa in his living quarters looking off into the distance. Lucifer strutted into the room, weaving in and out of Tejus's legs, purring obnoxiously. Tejus absent-mindedly patted him until the lynx curled up on his lap.

"Are you okay?" I asked him after a while. The silence was starting to get to me, and after we'd shared that experience in the cave, it felt strange that he was suddenly so distant and unapproachable.

"I'm fine," he said.

I wanted to tell him that what the hallucination had showed him wasn't real, that people did care about him... at least, I did... even if it was just a little.

61

"I saw everything," I murmured, "your brother falling from the tower, Jenus as a boy… all of it."

He looked up at me, his expression bleak.

"What do you mean?" he asked.

"I mind-melded with you. I could see what you saw."

I sat back in my seat. His expression was starting to frighten me—his hands clasped together so tightly that his knuckles were turning white.

"That's impossible. I tried to stop you seeing. You shouldn't have been able to do that… I thought you had gone."

"It was the hallucination, I think," I replied. "It stopped you from seeing or hearing me, maybe it stopped you from feeling my energy as well."

Now would have been a good time to tell him about the stone I'd stolen from the Hellswan sword, but I held back. It was crucial that I kept it in my possession—already it had helped us get back into the running for the trials, and were it not for stupid Queen Trina, we would be on par with Ash by now…what was she even doing here anyway, if the borders were up?

"Maybe," he agreed, but his brow was low and puzzled.

"Do you blame yourself for what happened to Danto?" I asked cautiously. I had been in the castle on the night that it had happened, right before the labyrinth trial that the Emperor had concocted for his sons. Tejus hadn't said a word about it—none of them had. They had gone to a very brief funeral in the morning, and then seemed to forget all about it while they fought for their chance to represent Hellswan in the kingship trials.

"No, of course not." He sighed. "Hazel, you need to forget everything that you saw in that cave. That liquid is potent. It works on the deepest subconscious of the mind, supplying fantasy that does not trouble me, nor *has* ever troubled me, in my waking life. Do you understand?"

I didn't believe him. The image of Danto had been on an almost continuous loop, and it wouldn't have been an image that Tejus would have been able to see with his own eyes, as the perspective was all wrong—which meant that he had imagined it, and who the *hell* wouldn't have something like that haunt them, whether they thought they were to blame or not? I didn't understand why Tejus had to keep himself closed off all the time – did he think it was a weakness that he cared for his brother, that he mourned his death? The idea seemed absurd to me.

As I looked at his unapproachable figure – the constantly tense muscles of his frame and the weary way he smoothed his forehead back with his hand, I felt a sudden and strong desire to try and get through to him. To at least *try* and connect with him on a level that was more human.

"Okay, I'll forget what I saw. But I want you to know something." I paused, trying to find the right words. "You're not alone, I—"

"Leave it!" Tejus bellowed suddenly, so loudly that Lucifer scampered into the next room.

"*Fine*," I bit out. "We'll just sit in silence with you brooding, as per usual, and me wondering how we're ever going to win the trials when Ash is so far ahead!"

I rose from the sofa, getting into the swing of my mini-rant, overwhelmed by a sudden and unaccountable anger. Obviously he didn't *want* to make any kind of connection with me. Where I saw Tejus as an almost friend, he clearly just saw me as a tool to help him win the trials. I thought we'd gotten beyond that - since our mind-melding had developed into something much more personal and intimate than him merely syphoning off my energy - but apparently I was wrong.

It hurt.

"And *who* is that woman who keeps cheering for him anyway?" I exclaimed, trying to focus on the trials alone, and not my increasingly conflicted emotions. "We would have won the trial if it wasn't for her, she's been biased from the beginning! Why isn't anyone saying anything – why is she even in the kingdom?" I stood with my hands on my hips, facing Tejus. I wanted answers.

"They don't defy her because she's a very powerful queen. Her kingdom is one of the most powerful in Nevertide. She holds a lot of sway over the ministers, but as for her preference for Ash, I couldn't tell you why," he replied, his voice much quieter, his eyes not quite meeting mine.

"Why is she even *at* the trials then? If she's from a different kingdom, why is she even here – what's she got to do with the outcome of the Hellswan trials?" I asked.

"The trials are a spectator sport. Anyone can witness them – all of the royal kingdoms have at least one minister present to report back on the progress, who were permitted access before the borders went up. It's more imperative to them now than ever before, with the imperial trials happening as soon as the kingship trials are concluded – they all want to know what they'll be up against. Queen Trina is permitted to be more… vocal, as she holds more sway than the others."

"And her obvious dislike of you? Do you know why that is?" I demanded.

"No."

I huffed. He was lying to me, I was sure. I just didn't know why.

Perhaps it's a good thing he didn't win the honesty trials, I thought. Tejus might be able to face his own truths, but he certainly had no problems lying to me.

I felt better about keeping the stone a secret from him. Clearly we each had limits to how open we could be with one another, and if he wasn't going to tell me why we were at such a disadvantage, then I wasn't going to share our one and only advantage—my secret weapon.

Benedict

The sleeping bodies on the floor meant that every time I needed the bathroom, I'd have to first complete an obstacle course—avoiding stepping on hands and feet, or waking anyone in the process. We had thirteen kids with us now, mostly around my age, but some were younger, and they usually slept in Ruby's room. We'd given them beds out in the living room, but every night they would make their way into her bedroom and nestle themselves at the foot of her bed, fighting for space. I supposed Ruby provided them a bit of adult reassurance.

Yelena tossed in her blanket as I stepped over her. She had originally been given one of the actual beds because she was one of the first, but had given it up for another kid who was malnourished and worse for wear—like she was aiming for sainthood or something.

"Hey, you up already?" Julian hissed at me from our bedroom.

"Yeah, I couldn't sleep… going to the bathroom," I whispered back, wincing as Yelena tossed again. I hadn't been sleeping well since we got here, and the nightmares of that horrible corridor and that stupid stone came every single night without fail.

I *hated* this castle.

"Wait." Julian yawned. "I'll come with you."

Julian and I had stopped using the bathroom in our quarters a few days ago. Ever since the other kids arrived there was always a line and it smelled weird—I guessed from the combined odors of sixteen people all constantly using it and only Jenney ever bothering to clean it up properly.

We pushed against the doors quietly, Julian in no more hurry to wake the others up than I was.

"Are the kids keeping you up?" Julian asked.

"No, not really—just dreams." I yawned loudly. "This place just generally gives me the creeps, I guess."

Julian nodded. "I can't wait to get out of here. There

are only four more trials to go, and they seem to be happening daily. It shouldn't be long now. *If* they stick to their word."

After we nodded a 'hello' to the guards posted outside our door, we continued our way along the corridor. The guards had given me an idea though.

"You know, I was thinking. We've got a bit of an army back there… all the kids, I mean. I know they're not up to much, but maybe we could become, like, a *team* or something… learn to protect ourselves from the sentries, and make sure we're armed at all times so we don't get kidnapped again."

Julian was silent for a moment, then said, "That's actually a good idea. I've been wondering what will happen once the trials are over. I mean, I know we were promised freedom, but what if the sentries decide they want to keep us? Who's going to stop them, right?"

I nodded. We only had the word of two sentries—and neither of them were that trustworthy. I kind of got the feeling that Ash was only promising Ruby whatever she wanted because he fancied the pants off her, and with Tejus—well, he just wanted to use Hazel to win.

"I bet they have a load of old swords and armor here," I continued. "We could train them to sword fight—in secret—and then we'd always be prepared for whatever they threw at us."

"I should speak to Jenney, see what she can find around the castle," Julian said.

"Yes, and we should think of a name, like a group of vigilantes or something, like the multiplayer teams in *Hell Raker*... something cool."

"Well, no one here will have heard of it. Why not just call ourselves the Hell Rakers? It's no sillier than the Hellswans," Julian concluded.

I nodded in agreement.

I briefly imagined us charging the sentries, a team of thirteen kids behind us, brandishing swords and dressed in the heavy chain mail I'd seen decorating some of the hallways of the castle, our faces marked with war paint, our cries heroic...

"Do you need the bathroom?" Julian prompted. I'd barely noticed that we'd reached our destination.

"Oh, yeah," I murmured and hurried inside—for once eager to get the day started.

* * *

After Julian and I had scarfed down a quick breakfast, we retraced our steps to the huge and disused chamber that we'd come across weeks ago in our search for Hazel—whom we'd believed was being locked away in the towers somewhere against her will.

We were unable to locate Jenney that morning, so, taking matters into our own hands, we decided that room was our best bet. It had been filled with broken furniture and large, dusty chests—we hoped that some form of weaponry might be contained within them. Rusty and broken swords would be fine for training purposes until we could get our hands on newer blades.

"I think this is it." Julian pointed toward a large door ahead of us.

Though we'd only come across the door in the gloom of night previously, there was something familiar about the large, ornate doorknob and the peeling varnish of its wood.

Julian pushed against it, and the door creaked open. We slipped inside after checking to be sure no one was following us—so far we seemed to have free rein over the castle, but I didn't want to test that theory.

Inside we saw our old footprints—the only evidence of anyone entering the room in years—crossing the room to the equally large door on the other side. We surveyed the ramshackle mess of the room, and, mixed in with the furniture, broken wood and sheet-covered paintings, there were four chests that looked promising.

"I'll take this one"—I pointed to the largest chest near us, and then pointed again to the second largest in size at the other end of the room—"and you take that one."

There was a large bolt on the chest, but no padlock to hold it in place. I bent the metal of the lock back and heaved it open.

I sighed.

"Nothing here but sheets," I alerted Julian with disgust. "Sheets and blankets."

I heard Julian heaving open his chest, and then only silence followed.

"What is it?" I asked, alerted by the lack of response.

"You've *got* to come and see this," Julian whispered, his voice filled with awe.

I hurried over and peered into the chest. Then blinked. It was full to the brim with gold objects—chalices, headpieces, pots, small figurines—and below them lay hundreds and hundreds of gold pieces.

"Wow," I whispered.

Julian let out a low whistle.

I picked up one of the pieces, and held it up to the light that streamed in through the windows. It was minted with strange symbols that *almost* looked like runes, but were more likely an early form of letters, although they weren't written in any discernible order. I could only recognize one symbol, and that was a dagger, centered in the middle of the coin.

"These look really *old*," Julian marveled. "I wonder how long sentries have been living here?"

I shrugged. "No idea, but these are medieval… but then again, this whole place feels like it's stuck in the Dark Ages…"

I tossed the coin back in the chest. It was an interesting find, but it didn't get us any closer to the weapons we were looking for.

"I'm taking some," Julian whispered, looking around the room shiftily as he shoved the gold into his pocket.

"That's stealing!" I admonished, though I felt kind of ridiculous doing so. We had been kidnapped after all.

"Stealing off sentries—I *really* don't have a problem with it," he retorted.

It was fair enough, but I didn't feel comfortable taking anything myself. With the stone dream never far from my mind, I was wary about picking up things in this castle that didn't belong to me.

"Let's look in the other chests," I suggested, already moving to the two other chests we hadn't explored yet. I opened one, and then accidentally dropped the lid with a thunderous *thwack* as I realized it contained musty-smelling clothing.

"Keep it down!" Julian hissed at me, jangling like a janitor as he walked over, his pockets bulging with coins.

I ignored him and opened the next one.

Finally.

"Bingo!" I announced, and lifted a broadsword by the hilt. It looked like it was made of bronze, and so old and used there were chips in the blade. But it was good enough.

Julian peered over the top of the chest.

"Awesome," he exhaled, leaning in to pick up a large mace.

"Okay." I put down the sword. "There's easily enough weapons in there for all of us—but how are we going to get them past the guards and into the living quarters?"

Julian looked about the room, and his eyes lighted on the first chest I'd seen, still standing open.

"We can wrap what we need in blankets, just tell the guards that it's extra bedding, if they even ask," he replied.

It seemed like a good plan. We took out fifteen swords, and I persuaded Julian to put the mace back. We put them into piles of three swords each, and rolled them up tightly into the blankets. Once we were finished I loaded up Julian's arms with as many as he could carry, and took the rest myself. Our piles were so high we could barely see over them, but we managed to open the doors and slowly made our way back to the rooms, both alert and tense that we might be stopped at any moment.

Miraculously, we didn't come across any ministers or castle staff, and I breathed a sigh of relief when we saw the guards standing outside our living quarters.

"You all right with those?" one of them asked kindly, but with bewilderment.

"Yeah, fine," I squeaked, "just extra bedding for the kids."

"Jenney gave it to us," Julian joined in.

The guard nodded, nonplussed, and opened the doors to let us inside.

We did it!

As soon as the doors closed behind us I grinned at Julian, our eyes alight with our unexpected success.

"All right," Julian announced to the room of listless kids, "we've got work to do today."

They stared back at us, uninspired and tired-looking. I found it difficult to believe that any of these children could have been much help to the sentries—they didn't look like they had any energy in them whatsoever. I felt that Hell Rakers might have been too optimistic a name for our current band of warriors.

"We're going to start training," I continued, taking over from Julian as he started to unwrap our loot. "The sentries have had the upper hand long enough. We don't know for sure if Ash or Tejus will get us out of here, so we need to take matters into our own hands. We're starting a secret society—we're going to dedicate ourselves to preparing for an all-out battle with the sentries."

Some of the children gasped and looked horrified, cowering behind each other as if a stampede of blood-thirsty sentries were going to come bursting through the door at any minute.

"Look, it might not come to that," I reassured them hastily. "This is more of a protective measure, so that we're all ready for anything. We're going to call ourselves the Hell Rakers—and we're going to be a force to be reckoned with."

"What, like that stupid game?" Yelena piped up. Apparently Yelena *had* heard of our favorite video game.

"No!" I retorted angrily. Trust her to ruin *everything*. "Well, a bit like that—but it's a good name."

She shrugged at my outburst and wrinkled her nose.

"Whatever. Seems a bit stupid to me. How exactly are we going to do all this preparation?"

"With these," Julian said, brandishing one of the more impressive-looking swords in our armory.

The kids oohed in wonder as the sword glinted in the light. Even Yelena looked marginally impressed, and stopped her whining for a few brief seconds.

"We're going to train in one of the deserted courtyards," I said. "Julian and I can wield a sword, and we'll show you guys how to do it too."

There was a lot of muttering from the kids, and I felt a wave of frustration. We were trying to empower them— you'd think they'd be a bit more excited.

"Everyone get a sword," I commanded. "There's more than enough. If you're small, go for one of the shorter ones."

They all lined up wordlessly now, and Julian handed out the swords one by one till everyone was armed.

Instantly there was a shrill shriek as one of the boys poked another.

"No messing around!" Julian yelled at them. "They might look old but they're still lethal. No waving them around until we're in the practice yard."

Finally, each of the kids stood in the living room,

armed, but certainly not deadly. At least they'd stopped treating it all like it was some game. They all stared back at Julian and me with wide eyes and solemn expressions.

Luckily, we were all wearing old sentry robes or loose jackets given to us by the servants—all large enough to conceal the weaponry till we found an appropriate place to practice.

"Right, all form a line, and place your weapons, carefully, inside your cloaks. We need to be able to get past the guards and any other—"

Julian broke off as Jenney entered the room, carrying a laundry basket and looking at us with an incredulous expression.

"What in the name of Nevertide are you all *doing?*" she asked.

"Um..." Julian flushed and lowered his sword down by his side as if it was nothing more out of the ordinary than a tennis racket. "Well, we thought we might try some sword training, in case we come up against the sentries, so we're prepared..." He trailed off into silence.

I sighed.

"Jenney, we're forming an anti-sentry group—in case Ash or Tejus go back on their word," I explained. "You need to *promise* that you won't tell them what we're doing."

"Right," said Jenney, looking more and more perplexed by the second, "but what do you think you're going to be able to do with swords against the sentries and their powers? They'll just give you such a bad headache that you'll crumble, crying, to the floor."

I looked at Julian, who blushed an even deeper shade of red. I guessed we'd been kind of stupid.

"Well—it's the best we've got," I reasoned. "We don't *have* mind powers, so there's little else we can do."

Jenney stood silent for a moment, then put down the basket.

"There are ways you can… *strengthen* your mind against them, like putting up blocks so they find it harder to get a grasp on you. Obviously it doesn't make a difference with a really powerful sentry, one who's determined to suck the life out of you, but it can be a deterrent against someone who's not that focused—like in battle, or something," she replied. "I can help you if you like?"

I glanced at Julian, who looked interested.

"All right," I said, "that could be good. But I think we should do sword fighting as well."

Mind-blocking and sword fighting combined would be a deterrent for sure. And plus, I wasn't willing to admit that my and Julian's plan had been completely hopeless… while we were stuck in this weird dimension, we needed all the help we could get.

BENEDICT

Jenney's methods of mind strengthening had been exhausting. At first I'd been skeptical—when she'd explained it to us it had sounded pretty easy, more like meditation than anything else, but the actual practice had been near impossible. Trying to empty our minds of everything and focus on one item or thought was a lot more difficult than it sounded. Julian had given up halfway through and stormed off to our bedroom to practice some sword moves, but I had continued, despite my fatigue and my own frustrations with the exercise.

I had an ulterior motive above just mind strengthening. I thought that maybe, if I mastered the art of clearing my mind, I might be able to send away the nightmares that had been a constant issue since Julian and I had stumbled across that narrow corridor in the castle. Every time I went to sleep, it was there... waiting for me.

Tonight I felt the same cold dread I did every night. Everyone else had long since begun to sleep, and I could hear the gentle snoring or soft mumbles drifting from the living room into the bedroom that Julian and I shared.

Julian slept like a log. I envied his dreamless sleep—there was enough going on in our day-to-day lives in Nevertide without spending my dreams here too.

Staring at the ceiling, I tried to practice what Jenney had taught us earlier in the day. I breathed in for five counts, and out for five again. It left me feeling a bit lightheaded, but I repeated it, trying to focus on the flame of a candle that she'd placed in front of each of us earlier. I could picture it clearly, and tried to train my mind to focus on that alone. I felt my eyelids grow heavy, and exhaustion washed over me. Eventually I succumbed to it, and drifted off.

Once again I was walking slowly down a darkened corridor, my heart thundering in my chest and my skin prickling with cold fear. It was a different corridor this time—larger, less obscured from the rest of the castle.

Vulture heads smirked down at me from the walls, laughing at me, the blank bone sockets of their eyes gleaming with malice.

There was hardly any moonlight—clouds shrouded all but a tiny glimmer, and there were no stars peering from the night sky. I kept walking, wanting with all my heart to turn back, but knowing that I *must* go on, driven against my will by some unknown entity that controlled every step I took, closer and closer to the large doors at the end of the corridor.

When I reached the doors, my trembling hand shot out, my palm resting on the cold, dead wood.

No, please, no. I don't want to go in there!

But my hand pushed against the groaning weight, and eventually the door opened wide enough for me to see inside. I stood trembling, rooted to the spot and unable to take another step.

I knew where I was.

All the furniture had been covered in dust sheets, but I recognized the layout of the room from when the servants had escorted Ruby here. We'd only had a brief glimpse as she was ushered in and we were moved on to our own sentries, but I was sure, on seeing the huge scythe at the far end of the room, that these quarters had once belonged to Danto.

A breeze blew in from the largest window, serving as a grotesque reminder of how he had met his end.

I hesitated at the door, my fear and desire to turn away fighting with the horrid, sick feeling of being pulled into the room. I wanted to slam the door shut behind me and never venture to this part of the castle again.

Unable to enforce my own will, I took a step into the room, and then another. It felt like someone was watching me as I stood alone in the room, the breeze rustling the tapestries on the wall, making them whisper dark thoughts to me.

My gaze became fixed on the stone floor. An embroidered rug lay over it, worn with age. In the middle of the rug there was a slight rise, one I wouldn't have noticed had it not been for the strong urge I felt to look at it—as if it were the only thing in the room.

I walked over to the edge of the rug and pulled it up from the corner. It was heavy and dusty, but I drew it back as far as I could and saw that where the rise had been, there was a wooden trap door built into the floor.

It had no lock, and I pulled at the iron ring to lift it. It opened easily, and I *knew*, without understanding why, that the trapdoor had been waiting for me—maybe for thousands of years… waiting for me to come and open it.

Steep steps led from the entrance down to the gloom beneath, but beyond that I could see the faint glow of sickly greens and pinks and reds.

The stones.

They called to me like they had in the corridor where I'd first come across them, their dancing light beckoning me forward so I had no other choice but to follow. I walked slowly down the steps, my legs feeling like they were about to collapse beneath me and my breath coming out in ragged gasps.

Please…

I offered up a silent plea—more than anything in the world I wanted to get the hell out of there. But my body kept moving forward, and eventually I was faced with another wall inlaid with the eerie, glowing stones.

Just like before, one of them started to shake and hum with energy, worming its way out of its socket and falling to the floor. It rolled toward me, slowly but still vibrating, as if it was some fat slug withering on a pile of salt.

No!

With everything I had, I fought the urge to bend down and pick it up. The whispers from the room grew louder— now they were like a deafening high-pitched whine in my ears, coursing through my temples.

Run! Run, NOW!

I turned, hands covering my ears, and ran back up the steps. Back in the room I slammed the trapdoor shut, and, without bothering to conceal it again with the rug, I pulled at the door.

The hallway lay ahead of me, now moonlit and brighter than it had been before. I could see torches burning off in the distance. I was safe… I was safe.

My stomach lurched, and the floor came up to meet me.

I came to with a start, gasping for air as if I'd just been submerged underwater. I could feel the sweat pouring down my back, and slowly became aware of my surroundings—the pinky glow of sunrise just starting, and the familiar walls of our living quarters. I was now standing—standing over Yelena, who lay fast asleep, tossing fitfully. The strangest thing was that my arms were stretched out , palms down… hovering over her body.

What the hell am I doing?

Hastily I placed them back by my sides.

"Benedict?"

I looked up to where the voice had come from. Jenney stood by the door to the servants' quarters, staring at me.

"What are you doing?" she asked softly.

"Nothing," I replied hastily. "What are *you* doing, snooping around?"

She raised an eyebrow at me, looking stunned at my rude reply.

"Well, I'm collecting the bloody laundry, if you must know, because it doesn't look like anyone else around here is going to do it!"

She strode back out of the door before I could stop her, slamming it in her wake.

I looked back down at Yelena, still sleeping, but more calmly now. I felt acid building up at the back of my throat, and the same sick, queasy feeling I'd had in my dream.

I was doing something very wrong here, but I had no idea what it was.

RUBY

"Are you ready?" Ash called from outside my bedroom. I had just finished dressing in my sentry gear, and had noticed a crowd forming below in the grounds of the castle.

"Yeah, come in," I answered, watching the red-robed sentries milling about near the portcullis.

"Do you think the trial's happening somewhere in the castle?" I asked Ash when he entered. He came to stand next to me, and together we looked out over the crowd.

"Certainly looks like it. Only one way to find out."

He led the way back into the living quarters, looking around at all the makeshift beds. We picked our way through the piles of bedding and reached the front door. Ash pushed against it, and the guards opened it the rest of the way, smiling at Ash as if he was their own personal hero.

"Hello, Ashbik. Good luck today." One of them grinned. "Show that Hellswan what you're made of." They both merrily thumped him on the back, and then we continued our journey to the entrance hall.

Once we arrived, the crowds almost swamped us. Ministers hurried to and fro, and along either side of the hallway merchants had set up stands—fruits, nuts, strange-smelling drinks—everything the spectators could possibly want to make their experience at the trials more enjoyable. I felt disgusted at how opportunistic they were being.

"Don't you think that's a little... tasteless?" I hissed at Ash as we passed a gnarled old man selling wood-whittled figurines of the champions.

Ash gave a short bark of laughter. "I suppose so, but it doesn't bother me. We don't have your TV sets, remember? We've got to enjoy the entertainment when it comes around."

As we jostled through the crowd, I could see the back of Hazel's head, and Tejus looming next to her. I kept my eyes on them, hoping that they might have more information about the location of the trial.

"Do you think Tejus gets a heads-up?" I asked Ash, the thought just occurring to me. Obviously the ministers wanted Tejus to win, and I wondered if this went as far as letting him in on vital information about the trials.

"I don't know." Ash frowned. "I've been looking for signs, but when it came to the unity trial he was just as bewildered as the rest of us. I don't think the ministers would go so far as to cheat outright... They tend to be more 'bend the rules' kind of people, not break them completely."

I thought back to the honesty trial and how the minister of ceremonies had tried to ignore the advice of Queen Trina and the watcher, and thought that Ash might be being a bit optimistic.

We finally escaped the hallway and entered the courtyard. It was no less busy here, but the air wasn't so overwhelmed with spices and roasting meat.

"Champions this way!" called out a minister, waving a large black flag to get our attention.

Ash led the way as the crowds started to part to let us through. There were lots of well-wishers on either side of us, and not just cheering Ash either. They called my name too, shouting words of encouragement. I was glad for it. As the trial neared, I felt the familiar knot of anxiety building up in my stomach.

The champions formed a small line in front of the minister. I counted only seven left of the twenty champions who had started. I was taken aback by how many had been knocked out in the previous trials. I hadn't been concentrating on the others, just obsessively keeping track of Ash's and Tejus's scores.

Tejus was standing at the front of the line, and we were standing at the back. The minister lowered the flag, and beckoned us to march forward. We were flanked on either side by red-robed watchers, who stared ahead, unflinching, and didn't make a sound.

The procession proceeded into another large courtyard of the castle, and then through yet another archway and courtyard, till we eventually entered a huge garden. It wasn't nearly as beautiful as the one Ash had taken me to—that one had been wild and lush, whereas this was carefully manicured with neat lawns and geometrical hedges.

We waited on a stone patio, the rest of the champions looking as baffled as I was about what the next trial could possibly entail.

Soon, the crowd started to form behind us at the far end of the garden. There were no seats this time, so most were sitting on the lawns or finding places to perch on stone statues of vultures and bull-horses. They were waving flags and banners, most of them with Ash's name written on them.

Above us a huge balcony overhung the lawn, and as I backed to the end of the patio I could see the ministers and royals taking their seats. Among them was Queen Trina. She wore the same deep blue robes I'd seen her in previously, but today she was wearing an elaborate golden headpiece that entwined with her dark hair in delicate chains. She was a beautiful woman, but her face was so severe and uncompromising that I found her strangely repulsive.

I shook the thought away and turned back to Ash.

"How are you feeling?" I asked.

"Confident," he murmured, "though I've no idea why. I've just got a good feeling about this one."

"Good." I smiled, privately thinking that apparently today I'd be doing the worrying for both of us.

"Champions, welcome!"

The minister of ceremonies stepped forward onto the patio, standing between us and the gathered crowds in a spot where the royals and officials on the balcony could see him clearly.

"After the last two trials, we are taking a far gentler approach to today's proceedings, but it is no less vital and important." He wagged his bony finger at us. "It is paramount that our chosen king embodies *all* the qualities of great leadership. Along with traditional attributes of a king, those who rule Nevertide must be able to *create*, as well as command, in order that we can progress as a great civilization."

The crowd roared, and the minister looked around, pleased at the effect his words were having on the people. The ministers in the royal box looked as stone-faced as always, unmoved by his speech. Queen Trina just looked bored.

"At the end of the patio, you will each find a plot of earth. Within the earth is a plant, not yet grown; much like yourselves, it is waiting for the chance to bloom and prosper, to show Nevertide what it truly is. Champions, your task is to promote that growth—the winner will be the one who creates the most awe-inspiring and precious flower, a full bloom."

What?

I turned to Ash. "I don't understand a word of this," I

whispered. "What the heck is he talking about? How are you going to make something *grow*?"

Ash looked despondent but whispered back, "Mind power, of course. In lesser organisms, sentries can generate growth. I've never tried it before. It's a very old practice."

I looked around at the other sentries. Some looked as glum as Ash at the prospect, others were trying not to laugh at such an unheroic trial. Tejus looked as stone-faced as always, and I breathed a sigh of relief. I very much doubted the prince of darkness had ever taken the time to learn how to speed up the growth of a flower.

"The trial begins when the horn sounds. Take your places, champions!" the minister announced.

We all stepped off the patio, and I saw the small patches of brown earth cut into the perfect lawn—seven plots of earth, each about a foot wide and long.

"This is going to take a lot," Ash mumbled at me. "If it starts to hurt, or you get a headache or anything, just tell me."

He sat down in front of the plot of earth. All the other sentries did the same, while the humans sat down behind them, waiting to have our energy sucked until the miracle happened. I was still having a hard time believing that this could be done.

I looked over at Hazel. She caught my eye and shook her head in astonishment, then turned back to Tejus.

"Is there anything specifically I can do?" I asked Ash.

"No. I don't think so. Just try sending me as much energy as you can. I don't know how this is even going to work…" He trailed off into silence.

The horn sounded, low and long. The trial had begun.

Not long after, I felt Ash pulling on my energy. I kept pushing what I could outward toward him, but whatever I was providing didn't seem enough. Nothing was growing in his plot of earth, but his shirt was damp with sweat from the exertion, and his shoulders hunched over with fatigue.

Looking over at the other plots was only slightly encouraging. None of them had made any progress either. I could hear shuffling and yawning coming from the crowd. It was hardly the most entertaining spectator sport—basically the equivalent of watching paint dry. *Jeez.* Even I was drifting off.

I tried to re-focus. I pushed out another 'shove' of energy in Ash's direction, but it still felt futile. I wondered if I was taking the wrong approach. If this trial was about creation, then maybe I also needed to become a bit more creative.

The more powerful mind-melds that Ash and I had

shared were when we'd sent pictures and images across to one another. Maybe *that* was the approach I needed to take. The memory to share was easy. I pictured us back in the secret garden—the amazing flowers that we'd seen, the soft light and the brilliant greenery that had grown wild from every inch of space in the earth. I tried to incorporate the smells as well—the honeysuckle and jasmine fragrances, and the warm smell of the soil.

As I sent the memory out to Ash, I felt a returning echo of peace and tranquility floating from him. He sat up straight, and though the tension in his body was still there, it now seemed purposeful rather than hopeless.

I kept going with the image, and when I'd exhausted all that I could remember, I found myself imagining the picnic that we'd never had. I was so deep in my fantasy that I seemed to lose sight of the trial and everything around me except the solid, steadying breaths of Ash sitting in front of me.

In my head, we were sitting under the tree again, the grass covered in a blanket that I recognized from home. Ash was leaning against the bark, popping bright red strawberries in his mouth and smiling lazily over at me. The sun was warm on our faces, and a slight breeze kept tangling my hair. Ash leant toward me, offering out a berry. When I took it, the tips of our fingers touched, and for a short moment all I was aware of was Ash's skin against my own, and the electricity whirring around my body in response.

The fantasy broke. Hastily I returned to the pictures of the garden, focusing on the bright petals, back to feeding Ash inspiration.

I felt an excitement building up in him, traveling along the mental chain we were sharing. Startled, I opened my eyes and looked at the earth plot. It was no longer empty.

A thick stem, about a meter high, had grown out of the ground. It was bright green, with small leaves branching off and thin grassy tendrils that reminded me of sweet pea. At the top of the stem was a giant bud, green at the bottom, but moving into shades of pale colors at its tip.

I couldn't help but squeeze Ash excitedly on the arm. His cool hand closed over mine briefly in thanks, and then he returned to focusing on his unfinished plant.

Looking over at the other plots of earth, I was surprised, and dismayed, to find that Tejus's plant was growing just as well as Ash's—with a large bud, still unflowered, at the top of his equally high stem. Some of the others were almost there, with stems in place but without buds, and these I could see growing more clearly. It was incredible, like watching a nature video on fast-forward, a process that was usually so slow that it was barely perceptible to the human eye, was happening at unprecedented speed. I could only stare, marveling at the nuances of the sentries' power.

Ash's flower started to bloom.

The petals opened, agonizingly slowly, to reveal full, large petals—their hue starting at a brilliant white, then morphing into bright splashes of blue, strawberry reds, pinks and a light gold dusting of pollen dancing on each one. The stigma was a bright purple and turquoise blue, with dark black dots at its very top. I gasped in astonishment, and the crowd, now roused out of their boredom, took a collective intake of breath, and expelled it with 'ahhs' and 'oohs'.

I quickly glanced at Tejus's plot. His flower had bloomed just as brightly and brilliantly as Ash's. His colors were darker, midnight blues as opposed to Ash's bright ones, and blood reds, ochres and deep bronze gold hues.

How are they going to choose?

It struck me how subjective the entire thing was—who was to decide if Ash's was the more brilliant, or Tejus's? I looked from one to the other, and saw that the watchers were doing the same from the patio.

A sudden movement made me look over at Tejus's flower again. One of the petals seemed to be jerking and moving of its own will.

Maybe it's dying!

I watched, holding my breath, as the petal started to flutter in the breeze. It moved rapidly, back and forth, generating a slight hum in the air. Then I realized what it was.

A butterfly.

Its wings were as large as the petals that had held it, and after a few more flutters, it floated up in the air, dancing around the flower—showing the bright kaleidoscope of color that made up its form.

The crowd applauded. Even *I* wanted to applaud.

How on earth did he do that? I wondered. I remembered what Ash had told me—about lesser organisms being manipulated for growth. Had Tejus just managed to take a caterpillar catalyst and transform it into a butterfly at the same time as he grew the flower? I could think of no other alternative theory.

"Well!" The minister stepped forward in his spot on the patio, practically rubbing his hands together with glee. "I think there can be no mistaking who our champion is today! A profound example of sentry power—

spellbinding!" he enthused. "The winner of the trial is none other than Prince—"

"Hold on!" A cry came from the balcony, and Queen Trina Seraq leant over the baluster. "I think, esteemed minister, that you are being too hasty. Surely it is only luck which enabled Tejus to create the butterfly. His plant somehow managed to obtain a cocoon during the stem growing process, but this was not because of his skill *at all*—sheer luck!"

The minister looked openly enraged. "Any of the stems could have been blessed with a cocoon in their infancy, your highness, but few would have been able to accomplish what Tejus did, growing two things at once —it was skill that transformed the butterfly, not luck!"

"I believe that Ashbik could have done the same given the opportunity—his flower is equally as beautiful as Tejus's," the queen countered.

"Queen Trina, what is the meaning of this?" the minister shouted up to her, letting his professional grace slide. "Clearly Tejus is the champion!"

Without waiting for a reply, the minister beckoned two of the watchers over. Each of them whispered in his ear, and they conversed in hushed tones while Queen Trina paced up and down the balcony, her face like thunder.

I took Ash's hand again, and he clasped mine tightly.

Eventually the minister smiled, and my heart sank. We had lost.

"It is agreed," he announced, "this winner of this trial is Prince Tejus! Truly a magnificent performance." The minister bowed in Tejus's direction and I rolled my eyes. Why not just stick a Head Boy badge on him and be done with it?

The crowd clapped politely, their initial enamoredness at Tejus's feat dulled as they all realized that Ash would be second place, winning only ten points. He was still in the lead, but Tejus wasn't far behind.

It was luck!

I couldn't help siding with Queen Trina on this. I felt that Ash had been robbed of winning by circumstance and coincidence. It should have at least been another tie.

"I'm sorry, Ash," I muttered.

"Don't worry about it. It's the last win he's going to get… I promise you that." As Ash spoke, his eyes glinted with determination and resolve. I recalled his truth from the cave. *I am ruthless. I will stop at nothing to achieve my goals.*

I shuddered despite the warmth of the sun.

HAZEL

The minister held up his hands for silence after he'd confirmed that Tejus was the winner. I was so excited that we'd won that I could barely concentrate on what he was saying, but as the rest of the champions gradually fell silent, I caught the end of yet another speech.

"... and so, as we reach the halfway mark of the trials, a Champions' Feast will take place in the Hellswan castle, with Prince Tejus as our host. And all those taking part in the trials are expected to be in attendance, humans included."

I groaned inwardly. Another meal of dull food and whispering sentries. At least this time we'd all be there, and

Jenus thankfully wouldn't be in attendance; it wouldn't be too bad if Ruby and I could sit together and ignore the stares.

The champions rose from their positions on the floor, and I could see Nikolay approaching with an open smile on his face. I'd seen that his stem had grown, but not flowered, and so he'd been awarded only ten points. There was one sentry still sitting on the ground, staring at the soil of his patch, where not so much as a weed had grown.

"Congratulations," Nikolay said, "that was impressive. Your mind must be something else... I hope Tejus realizes how precious you are."

The last line was said in a low voice, and his gaze met mine.

"Well, he's certainly happy now," I murmured, looking around for Tejus' looming figure. I couldn't see him—which was odd. He never left my side when we were in public.

"They usually have dancing at these feasts," Nikolay continued. "Could I request a dance now, for later?"

"Uh." I suddenly felt anxious that Tejus wasn't around and wanted to find him. I smiled distractedly at Nikolay. "I guess..."

"That's of course if Tejus won't mind." He looked

doubtful for a moment.

"I'll see you at the feast." I backed away hurriedly.

Where is Tejus?

I scanned the sentries, their tall frames and cloaks all blending into one, but usually I could spot Tejus—he was slightly taller than most of them. If I was perfectly honest with myself, there was something about Tejus that always drew me closer, as if I was constantly overly aware of his presence even when faced with a sea of people, my subconscious instinctively sought him out. Perhaps it was the mind-melding. I wondered if sharing so much with someone had left its mark within me, so that we would never quite be fully apart. The idea was confusing – and unsettling.

I saw Ash and Ruby, moving back toward the castle, and noticed that it was the direction that everyone now seemed to be heading. Had Tejus gone on without me? It seemed highly unlikely.

I stood back from the patio, hoping that I could gain some perspective. Again I scanned the crowd, but found no Tejus-like presence. I looked up at the royal balcony, but it was empty.

I called his name self-consciously, and a few sentries looked over at me—but then continued on their way.

Forget it, I muttered to myself. I'd go and wait in his living quarters. He couldn't get mad at me if he'd been the one to leave me in the first place. I was about to walk forward when a low monotone voice caught my attention.

It was coming from a small cluster of trees, slightly off from the main patio and lawn, out of sight from the castle. I was sure that it was Tejus's voice that I was hearing, but there was another voice answering his that I couldn't quite place.

As silently as I could, I walked toward the trees. When I was close enough, the voices floated over more clearly and I could catch snippets of the conversation.

"You are making your bias so obvious!" Tejus spoke curtly, and I could imagine the clenching of his jaw. I knew that tone well.

Nothing but silence greeted his statement, and he continued, "What is it? I cannot even begin to understand this scheme of yours. To what end do you want the kitchen boy as the Hellswan king—and then would you put him in the running for emperor? Do you really believe that he has what it takes to lead Nevertide?"

I could now guess who he was talking to, but I wanted to confirm my suspicions. I edged closer to the trees and peered through the soft prickles of their ferns. I couldn't really see Tejus, as he was too close to where I was standing to be anything more than a black-robed figure, but the person he was talking to was easily identified as Queen Trina Seraq.

"You are so arrogant!" she hissed at him. "It is time the Hellswans stopped getting everything handed to them on a platter, or are you afraid of a little competition, Tejus?"

Tejus laughed cruelly. "This sounds like the ravings of a bitter woman. Did our parting hurt you so much that you're now bent on destroying my future as king?" His voice oozed with contempt.

Queen Trina looked as if he'd just punched her in the gut.

"How *dare* you! How dare you think so little of me that you assume my motive is petty revenge? Did what we have mean so little to you? Do you think so low of *me*?" she cried back at him, and I could see tears forming in her eyes. Whether they were from rage and frustration or genuine sorrow, I couldn't tell.

"You left me in that castle, alone with my miserable old father. Of *course* you hurt me, Tejus! The moment your father called on you, it was like I didn't exist. You chose your brothers, whom you *hated*, over me—and now you fawn over that stupid human girl like she's one of us. It's embarrassing for all sentries! Knowing all this about you, how would you assume that I would think *you* would prove to be a great leader?"

"Don't *you* presume to understand my feelings toward Hazel!" he retorted in disgust.

His outburst only resulted in silence. Queen Trina was breathing heavily and clutching her stomach, as if his words had physically whipped her.

Tejus's back stiffened. He wasn't saying anything, but it felt like he regretted the words that had escaped him.

What does he even mean?

What feelings? I wasn't aware that Tejus had any feelings toward me that he would need to defend with such vitriol...but maybe he was saying it to purposely wound Queen Trina.

Shoving my personal curiosity aside, I refocused on the scene before me. Tejus took a step toward the queen, and gestured helplessly as she remained turned from him— almost like a wounded animal, dreading the next attack of its predator.

"I didn't know how you felt," he muttered. "I... suppose I wasn't being perceptive enough to realize you were in pain. Why did you never say anything?"

"Would it have made a difference?" she scoffed.

Tejus paused before answering, and Queen Trina's face fell a fraction more.

"No," he replied stiffly. "It wouldn't have. But don't think it wasn't hard for me. I didn't like that the choice had to be made. And I don't want you to continue resenting my decision. What's done is done."

His voice was firm, but it wasn't without its own slight tinge of melancholy. I wondered what had gone on between the two of them—some sort of romantic relationship, that was obvious, but I just couldn't get my head around Tejus in that role… What kind of boyfriend would he have made? Was he different back then, before the trials and before the Hellswan brothers turned against one another?

Even the way he was speaking to Queen Trina was different to how he usually spoke to others. Though heated and angry and then bitter in turns, it sounded intimate— like I was intruding on their small, private world.

"Allow me my feelings, Tejus," Queen Trina warned him. "It doesn't affect my wishes for the outcome of the kingship. As you say, what's done is done."

"I don't believe you. What other reason could you *possibly* have?" Tejus retorted.

"Whatever the reason, it is my own. Let us leave it at

that."

She clutched her cloak tighter around her frame, and turned to leave. Tejus suddenly jumped into action, crossing the space between them in two short strides. He pulled her back by the upper arm and gripped her body to his.

For a moment I thought I was going to be subjected to even more intimacy between the former couple, and I felt bile rise at the back of my throat. But then I got a clear look at Tejus's face.

It was contorted in fury.

"I am sorry," he whispered in her ear. "But if you keep cheering on the kitchen boy and swinging the trial his way, I shall expose you as the attempted kidnapper of Hazel. So help me gods, I shall."

Queen Trina's face drained of color, and she struggled free of his grasp.

"You wouldn't dare!" she hissed.

Tejus spat back with a condescending laugh, "Don't test me, Trina."

She flounced off toward the border of trees, and I hastily scurried off toward the gate I'd seen everyone leaving through. I should have waited for Tejus, but I needed some alone time. My head was swimming with the information I'd just gleaned.

I hurried through the main hall, weaving in and out of the milling crowds and the food stalls, trying to find a part of the castle that would be quiet. I spied a small wooden door off the main hall and pushed against it. It opened into an empty corridor, and I slammed the door against the crowd.

In the silence I heard my breath coming in short rasps, and I leaned back against a stone wall.

Queen Trina was my attempted kidnapper.

When I had first heard her voice through the trees, high and taught like it had been in Tejus's room during her attempted kidnap, it had half-conjured up a memory – but I'd not been able to properly place it and had pushed the thought aside.

No wonder Tejus didn't care about finding the culprit.

I recalled the day that it had happened, and how afterward Tejus had connected with my mind to get a front-row seat to the events as they'd unfolded. Before I'd shown him what had taken place, he'd seemed desperate to find out the identity of my attacker—and I'd presumed it was so he could hunt them down and stop them. Afterwards, he'd completely backed off, changing the subject and ignoring the situation completely.

Well, at least now I know why.

I was furious with him. In the past Tejus had struck me as honorable, no matter what I thought of some of the particulars of his personality. But letting my attacker roam free when he knew who it was left me feeling utterly betrayed.

And lying about it!

Twice now Tejus had lied to me. First by keeping the identity of my kidnapper a secret, and then when I'd asked about Queen Trina and her obvious bias toward Ash.

Was he keeping their relationship a secret because Tejus thought I had no *right* to know about it, even though it clearly affected me? Or was he trying to protect her because he still had feelings for her?

I felt hot all over, my skin prickling against the silk of my sentry robes. I recalled the almost tender tone of Tejus's voice when he'd apologized for hurting her, and the admission that he had also found their separation hard.

I wondered how long they'd been together, and how serious the relationship had been. Judging by the dramatics of Queen Trina, I assumed that it had been fairly serious. Was *that* part of the reason that Tejus was the way he was—cold, distant and taciturn? Was she in any way responsible? Or was Tejus a different man entirely when he was in a relationship or—and I could hardly comprehend the idea—when he was in *love*?

Questions buzzed relentlessly in my head. Many that I suspected I would never get answers to.

One thing I knew for sure was that my captor was a greater enigma than I'd ever imagined, and that he was keeping secrets from me—important ones that could affect the outcome of the trials.

That makes two of us, I thought. I reached into my robes and felt for the stone. It was warm and tingly, inviting me to rub my fingers over its smooth surface and latch onto its immense power.

Taking a deep breath, I re-entered the bustling hallway. Tejus was a few yards away from me looking around the crowd. I closed my eyes briefly, and when I opened them I fixed a faux smile in place.

"Did you miss me?" I quipped.

RUBY

The coals of the fire were glowing warmly. Ash was dozing in one of the battered old armchairs and I was in the other. When the kitchen was cleared of all the servants, and the household staff had left for the day, this was still our favorite place to come. It was the only place in the castle where I felt truly comfortable, where the Hellswan family's presence was almost non-existent.

Ash stirred in his sleep, and then slowly opened his eyes.

"I dozed off?" he asked, looking around the darkened room and spying the dying fire.

"Almost the second you sat down," I confirmed with a smile. "At least you don't snore."

Ash yawned in response and stretched out his long physique. I curled my feet back under me on the chair and continued staring into the embers. It was late, but I didn't much feel like going to bed. Though the additional humans we were picking up at a rapid pace in our living quarters were sweet, and badly needed our care, I also needed a break.

"I was thinking about Queen Trina Seraq." Ash interrupted the silence.

"In your dreams?" I cocked an eyebrow questioningly.

"No!" He blushed. "Not like that. I was thinking about her behavior at the trials—how she keeps sticking up for me, and putting Tejus down. It's weird. I used to see her a lot around the castle. I thought that she and Tejus were close. Apparently not." He frowned and poked at the fire.

"Maybe she doesn't think he'll make a good leader." I shrugged. "It's not that weird. The Hellswans are hardly Nevertide's most popular family—look at how the crowd cheers for you!"

"Yes, but royalty usually stick with royalty. I don't trust her," he declared.

I thought Ash might be overacting a little bit, but I could see his point. I had noticed how strange it was that she stuck up for a kitchen boy. She was clearly royal blood after all—and the way she'd so passionately denounced Tejus's efforts today struck me as odd. But we also had a lot to thank her for. She was the reason Ash was ahead in the trials, and the sole reason that he'd won the disk trial.

"Well, I can't help but be a fan," I replied. "She's done a lot for us—no matter what her motives."

"Just be careful," Ash muttered darkly.

I was about to respond when Jenney peered around the kitchen door.

"Can I have a word?" she asked politely, looking at me.

"Sure," I said, dreading what messy incident had befallen the kids.

She entered the kitchen, and Julian came in behind her. They both looked strangely somber.

"Where's Benedict?" I asked hastily.

"That's who we've come to talk to you about." He held out his hands in a gesture to stop when I instantly jumped to my feet. "Nothing's immediately wrong… it's just… he's doing *weird* stuff."

"Like what?" I asked.

"Tell them." Julian nudged Jenney forward.

She looked at me with a worried expression on her face, chewing her lip.

"I don't know if it's anything serious—it's just that this

morning I think Benedict was sleepwalking, and I saw him standing over Yelena, one of the younger girls, with his palms outstretched... I wouldn't have thought anything of it, but it was the look of his *face*—like it wasn't him, just an empty shell."

Jenney shivered and pulled her shawl closer to her.

"Lots of people sleepwalk," I murmured. "Are you sure it wasn't just the shock of seeing him when he should have been asleep?"

What Jenney had just told me sent a cold chill running through my bones, but I wanted to check this story out before I jumped to any conclusions or overreacted. It potentially sounded like an overactive imagination. Sleepwalking tended to be far more unnerving for the people who witnessed it than for the sleepwalkers themselves. Benedict had never mentioned that it was something he did—but that didn't mean something was wrong. I knew that sleeping in a new house or a change of lifestyle could also bring on sleepwalking habits.

"Ruby, I've seen many strange things in this castle, and so I don't scare easily. I swear to you there's something wrong with Benedict. That face—that face wasn't normal."

I nodded. I trusted she believed what she saw.

"Julian?" I turned to him. "Have you noticed anything odd about Benedict?"

"Other than him looking tired and withdrawn and pale every day?" he replied. "You've seen that too, Ruby. We've all seen it, but we've ignored it. He's been complaining that he's not getting enough sleep. I'm worried that something's seriously wrong."

He was right. I had noticed that Benedict didn't look well, but he'd shrugged off my concerns and I had been so preoccupied with the trials that I hadn't pursued it.

"Have you told Hazel?" I asked. "She needs to know. We all need to understand what's going on."

Julian shook his head, face flushed with annoyance. "We can't find her anywhere—and we're banned from Tejus's living quarters. She's too wrapped up in the trials anyway."

"That's not fair," I replied sharply. "You haven't given her a chance."

Julian shrugged, not bothering to reply.

Just then the door to the kitchen swung open again. Benedict sauntered into the kitchen, stopping dead when he saw us all looking back at him in silence.

"What?" he asked, confused.

"Um… nothing—what are you doing still up?" I asked.

He looked at me strangely. "Getting a glass of water?"

Oh.

He filled up his glass from the nearest jug, and held it toward us.

"Now I'm going to bed," he announced. "See you bunch of weirdos in the morning."

Julian

I didn't understand why it was necessary for Benedict and me to attend the Champions' Feast. It was probably my fault. Since I'd told Ruby that there was something wrong with Benedict, she had insisted that we were both within eyesight most of the time—except when she was off with Ash, doing that weird mind-meld thing, which, as far as I could tell, entailed looking deep into each other's eyes and then sitting in silence with blissed-out expressions on their faces.

I thought it was creepy.

Jenney had gotten excited about us going though, and found some brand-new sentry robes to dress us in. Which was why Benedict and I were standing in boxers and t-shirts in the middle of the living room while the other kids snickered. It was hardly *Hell Raker* material.

"Lift up your arm, Julian, I need to wrap the robe a bit—it's too long," Jenney commanded.

She wrapped the silky material around me and then tied the robe once at the back and then again at the front.

"Have a look!" she exclaimed, dragging an old mirror over that she'd found especially for the occasion.

"You look ridiculous," Benedict deadpanned.

"So will you in a minute," I retorted. "Can you start on him now?"

Jenney rolled her eyes at us, then took the second robe off the sofa. She started to dress Benedict while I sniggered at him.

Yelena walked in from the bathroom and began laughing.

"Isn't that a bit big for you?" She gestured at the robe that fell past Benedict's feet and swamped his body completely.

"Yelena, that's not helpful," Jenney chastised her.

"What are you doing here anyway?" Benedict scowled at her. "Shouldn't you *all* be practicing your mind strengthening?" He glared at the kids sitting round the living room, ogling us and snickering.

Yelena rolled her eyes and flung herself on the nearest sofa. Benedict had a problem with her, but I didn't really get it. I thought she was quite funny.

"Okay, I think you're ready." Jenney stood back and surveyed us both. Benedict looked better—she'd managed to pin in the extra material, so neither of us looked quite as ridiculous as everyone was hoping we would.

"So what's the deal?" I asked Jenney. "Do we just march on down there? Or do we need to wait for Ruby and Ash?"

She shrugged. "I'm not entirely sure. Humans, other than Hazel, have never been invited to an official dinner before."

"I say we go solo," Benedict replied. "We got invited after all. I don't want to hang around here all evening waiting till Ruby decides she's ready. Girls her age can take a lifetime."

It was a fair point. I just wasn't sure how prepared I was to face a room full of sentries. Jenney had been working us hard on the mind strengthening, but I didn't seem to be making much progress. I kept returning to the swords, knowing deep down that it was all pretty futile. If a sentry wanted to delve into my brain and leech out my energy then there wouldn't be a whole lot I could do about it. The thought was depressing.

"Well, if you're so eager to get down there, lead the way." I relented.

"Don't forget that I'll be around. When you enter the main hallway, you'll see a small door at the far end, opposite the arches. If anything happens, or if you need me, just go through that door. It will lead you straight to the servant quarters," Jenney instructed. "Just try not to annoy anyone."

She glared at me when she said it, but I didn't need the reminder. I wasn't about to go and piss off a bunch of sentries just for the hell of it.

"Good luck!" Yelena said merrily, waving at us both. I waved back, but Benedict just glared at her. Her face fell momentarily when she caught his look, and she looked lost for a moment.

"You have *got* to be nicer to her," I hissed at him. "What's your problem?"

"Nothing! She's just really annoying. She thinks she knows *everything*," he retorted. "It's always 'no, Benedict, this way; Benedict, that's a stupid name; blah, blah, blah,'" he mimicked in a high-pitched voice. "Ugh."

I sighed. I might not get what his deal was, but at least he looked a bit more alive today—he didn't look as zombiefied as he had recently.

"How are you sleeping, has it gotten any better?" I asked.

Benedict groaned again. "I wish everyone would stop asking—first Jenney, then Ruby and now you. I'm *fine*."

"We're just worried about you. You haven't been the same since we found that stupid corridor. Do you still dream about it?"

"Will you just drop it!" Benedict huffed angrily. "I said I'm fine—I'm *fine*."

"Okay, okay… keep your shirt on," I muttered. *Fine, my ass.* But I dropped the subject. We were nearing the hall anyway, and I could hear a band tuning up and chairs being dragged back and forth across the stone floor.

A black-robed sentry stood waiting at the entrance, and he raised his eyebrows at us as we approached.

I hesitated, not sure what the protocol was.

"Um, hello. We're Benedict and Julian."

The sentry nodded, and slowly looked us up and down. His face broke into what I assumed was meant to be a smile, but came out as a sickly grimace.

"Yes." He nodded. "You're to sit with your fellow humans, but they haven't arrived yet. They'll be using the champions' entrance."

He gestured to the arched columns that stood at one end of the room.

"You should stand to the side for now, and then sit when they've been seated."

We both nodded and stood where he'd indicated—by the side of the wall. At least we got a good view of the last-minute preparations. I'd never seen any part of the castle look this opulent and lavish.

The vulture heads that lined the circumference of the room were almost completely obscured by large wreaths of tree boughs, and the air smelt of pinecones and fresh air. Candles were lit on every available surface, and the banqueting tables themselves, which were easily long enough to seat a hundred each, were covered in an ivy-type plant that ran the length of them and entwined in the gold and silver goblets and tableware.

I'd been right about the band. A group of plain-clothed sentries were setting up in the corner, near the small wooden door that Jenney had told us was the servants' entrance. They were tuning the type of instruments I would have expected at a medieval feast—objects that looked like lutes and harps.

"I feel like we've gone back in time a couple of centuries," I whispered to Benedict.

Soon an influx of ministers arrived and all started to take their seats at the tables. They spoke in low tones, muttering constantly between themselves. They certainly didn't look like they were in a feast kind of mood. Most of their faces wore the same dour expression I'd always seen.

The band started to play a low, warbling song and the ministers' murmurings became hushed. When the band stopped, one of the ministers stepped forward from behind the archways.

"Welcome! All of you. As most of you know, tonight we are gathered to celebrate the halfway point of the trials, and to commend the champions who have participated in the trials thus far, and the ones who continue to do so. Our host, Prince Tejus of Hellswan, thanks you all for coming, and hopes you all have a wonderful evening ahead."

The ministers rapped their knuckles on the table in appreciation. It made me think of some secret sect where they had special handshakes and rituals that involved slaughtering baby goats.

The minister started to announce the champions. He began with the ones who had already been knocked out— these came without their humans, but were seated to a round of short table-rapping from the ministers. The defeated champions looked downcast as their names were read out, bowing once and then proceeding to their assigned seats.

Eventually the minister reached the champions who were still in the running. They strode proudly through the archways to applause from the already seated champions. Apparently most would be putting the competitive spirit behind them tonight, but I wondered how well Ash and Tejus would manage that.

"Next up is Ashbik, and his human Ruby! Ashbik is currently in the lead with seventy points!" the minister exclaimed, though it sounded forced and hollow. Whenever Ash entered the trial fields the applause was deafening. In a room mostly full of ministers, the applause was nothing more than a polite flurry.

"Wow. They really don't like him, do they?" Benedict whispered.

Before I could reply, the sentry who had been at the door walked over to where we were standing.

"You can sit with your fellow human now," he said, indicating at the chairs next to Ruby and Ash. We both muttered our thanks and hurried to the seats, not wanting to stay in the sight line of the seated sentries for too long.

"You came!" Ruby whispered. "How are you both?"

"Okay," I replied, as Benedict turned to watch as Tejus and Hazel walked in.

"Last but by no means least is Prince Tejus Hellswan and his human Hazel. The prince is only twenty points behind Ashbik!" the minister announced grandly, and a large applause swept through the banquet hall.

Hazel saw us and waved, trotting over toward us so that Tejus had no other choice but to follow. He didn't look remotely pleased at the thought of sitting with us, but I doubted he ever looked particularly pleased about anything.

"Looks like we're both in the lead," Hazel muttered to Ruby.

"I think it's well deserved," Ruby replied, wetting her lower lip. "You can't deny though that the caterpillar *was* a lucky break."

Hazel nodded, but it was clearly half-hearted. I had known the two of them long enough to recognize when tension was brewing. And you could cut this one with a knife.

I looked over at Benedict. He looked worriedly back at me.

This was ridiculous. I had known the girls to argue over stupid things—who made the better James Bond, what was so-and-so's best album, who was better with the crossbow—but they were always short-lived and light-hearted. To be getting competitive over the trials, as if they mattered other than as a tool to get us out of here, was *so* dumb.

Are they really taking it so seriously?

"One more announcement before the feast starts." The minister clapped his hands for attention and addressed the room. "As you know, there will now be a few days' rest before the contest resumes. Use it wisely. During this time off, I have one small piece of advice for our champions, which is to *know your surroundings* in preparation for the next trial!"

Murmurs erupted from the table. The champions looked skeptical and I could understand why—it was hardly much to go on. Ash and Ruby started talking together in low voices, while Tejus and Hazel did the same. Their backs turned away from one another, and to me it so obviously symbolized the rift that was growing between us. It wasn't just the girls. With Benedict refusing to talk about what was going on, I felt that we were all drifting into our own, different experiences of Nevertide, and it wasn't a good thing.

The ministers' clue, *know your surroundings*, may not

have been that helpful for the champions, but it sparked an idea in me.

We had been so focused on waiting for the outcome of the trials and leaving our fate in the hands of the sentries that none of us had given proper thought to what *we* could do in the meantime. The team we'd assembled was all well and good, but it had quickly become a way to help develop counter-measures against the sentries in the event they might pose some harm later down the line. But what we hadn't done was taken any immediate action. Just because we'd tried to exit through one location within the kingdom, it didn't necessarily mean that the entire circumference of the boundary would be as strong as that one. Presumably it was the collective power of the ministers keeping it in place—but with the trials taking place and the disorder within the castle, who was to say that there weren't some areas where they'd been more lax in the upkeep of the borders?

"Benedict," I breathed into his ear so softly I could barely hear myself. "I've just had an idea… we should take the others out and check some of the areas where the boundaries might not be that strong. All we'd need is a map—then we can locate areas we think might be weaker."

Benedict looked doubtful. "It's a bit of a stab in the

dark, isn't it?"

"Well, yeah, but we should still try at least."

He shrugged. "I guess we can try. We shouldn't get our hopes up though."

I turned away from him before I said something I would regret. His lackluster response wasn't what I wanted to hear. It also wasn't the Benedict I knew—the kid who was up for anything, no matter how stupid, dangerous or ridiculous it seemed. He was back to his lethargic state again.

I stared dully at my plate. It had been filled with some grayish-brown gruel and looked like a science experiment gone wrong. I poked it unenthusiastically. Out of the corner of my eye I saw Hazel doing the same. She noticed me looking at her.

"How are the kids doing, Julian?" she asked, turning away from Tejus for a moment.

Before I could reply, one of the champions loomed over her shoulder. He was tall, like they all were, and not as broad as Tejus, with over-groomed hair.

"You look beautiful, Hazel." He leered down at her. "I've just heard that the band will be starting shortly. May I take the liberty of asking you for the first dance?"

What?

I waited for Hazel to tell him to back the hell off, but she *blushed* slightly and then... rose from her chair.

Are you kidding me?

Ruby and Ash was bad enough, but this was a step too far. Had we all completely forgotten that these sentries were the *enemy*?

I looked over at Tejus. The only consolation was that Hazel's acceptance had clearly infuriated him. His face was like thunder—he looked even more pissed off than he usually did.

A few seats down, Ash and Ruby were still stuck in their own little world. Benedict was staring into space, occasionally stabbing his gruel and looking lost.

I'd had enough.

I rose from my chair, but not one of them looked over at me. I wasn't going to sit here a moment longer and pretend that everything was okay—that we hadn't been kidnapped by a bunch of tall energy-sucking leeches who had then locked us in their dimension.

"I'll see you back at the room," I muttered to Benedict.

"See you," he murmured back, barely glancing in my direction.

There were crowds of ministers everywhere, so I avoided the entrance that we'd come in. Instead I made my way to the small servants' door. I passed Hazel on my way, encased in the arms of the champion as they danced. She was smiling at something he'd said, and didn't see me.

I tutted in disgust, and wove my way to the door.

Just as I approached it, Jenney came out carrying a gallon of liquid in both hands.

"Are you all right?" she asked, studying my face.

"No—no, I'm not all right," I replied angrily. "I'm sick to death of sentries. And *these* humans"—I gestured over to my friends—"are behaving like everything's okay. And it's *not*. The lot of them are leeches, sucking off us as if we're blood bags. I've had enough of it."

Jenney jerked her head back at the ferocity of my words.

"We're not all like that," she replied softly.

I belatedly realized that I'd just insulted her. But I was too angry to care.

"*Most* of you, then," I hissed.

She bit her lip and looked down at the floor. *Tough.* I'd upset her, but I wasn't in the mood to deal with her feelings—it wasn't like ours had ever been taken into account.

I stormed off through the door without looking back.

Hazel

I woke, bleary-eyed, to the greenish glow of the crystals in my blackout room. I'd had a strange dream last night, probably the result of drinking too much of the strange berry drink I'd been given at the banquet. I'd only had two glassfuls and I didn't think it was alcoholic, but its effect seemed akin to wine.

In my dream I'd been dancing with that guy Nikolay, just as we had been earlier on in the evening, but our surroundings were completely different—we had been in a moonlit garden, on a vast lawn which had an opulent marble fountain that we danced around. In the far distance there was a huge oak tree, and elsewhere on the lawn small clusters of trees in a circular pattern were growing intermittently a few yards apart. I'd stopped dancing, left Nikolay by the fountain and gone to look at them. When I peered through the branches of the first one, I found two snow-white swans circling on a small pool. In the second one, the pool was blood red, and the bodies of the swans floated on top of it. I rushed to the third tree cluster, and found the same. In a state of panic, I'd looked up at the oak tree in the distance. Tejus was standing beneath it, the Hellswan sword in his hand, its blade bright red.

There was a short rap on my door.

"Hazel, wake up." Tejus's short call was my good morning salutation.

I reluctantly emerged, and Tejus gave me some space to bathe and dress, and then consume some fresh fruit the servants had brought up to his living quarters. As I ate breakfast he sat opposite me, not taking a bite and watching me with barely concealed impatience.

"What's the plan, then?" I asked when I was finished.

"I want to take you somewhere," he replied shortly. "It may be of interest to you."

I was intrigued. No doubt there would be an alternate motive. The words of the minister last night rung in my ears—*know your surroundings.* But I was used to that by now. I only hoped this place would be out and away from the castle. The gray stone walls, matching a gray day, were starting to get to me.

"Is it outside?" I asked.

"Yes." He looked at me quizzically but I didn't elaborate. "Are you done?"

"I'm done."

He rose swiftly and led the way out of his living quarters and down into the main hall. The castle felt sleepy—there were fewer sentries than normal milling about, and I guessed that most of them would be sleeping off the effects of last night.

No such luxury for me.

"We will take a vulture," Tejus said as we entered the courtyard.

Ugh.

My stomach did a queasy flip. While the vultures were magnificent, flying on them scared the crap out of me—and it was an even less appealing prospect today.

We approached the cage where the royal vultures were kept. Tejus opened it up and took a step inside. The vulture he caught hold of was instantly docile, no doubt subjected to Tejus' mind power as the sentry pulled the humongous bird from the cage before closing the door behind it.

Tejus stroked the short feathers on its neck, while its great hooked beak bowed to the ground in greeting. I approached with more caution, unnerved by the beady black eye that watched me carefully.

"Ready?" Tejus asked. Without waiting for a reply, he wrapped his hands round my waist and lifted me onto the back of the bird. He launched himself up behind me in a single graceful jump. I felt only mildly more secure as he locked his arms around my waist.

"Stop fidgeting," he murmured.

"I can't help it! I feel like I'm going to fall off at any moment."

I couldn't see his expression but I could gather from the slight huff that he was irritated.

"You're not going to fall off," he replied in a more measured tone. "Just try to... enjoy it."

Enjoy it. That wasn't a very Tejus-like thing to say.

A second later the bird was in flight. I felt a few jolts as it got off the ground, and then the smoother sensation of its glide as the castle disappeared beneath us and Hellswan's landscape unfolded inch by inch as we rose higher in the air. From this height I could almost see the slight wavering and almost liquid-like motion of the barriers that covered the kingdom, blocking us off from the rest of (what I assumed was) the supernatural dimension.

We moved far away from the castle and its closest village, passing other sprawling buildings and hamlets that lay shadowed in the valley of a snow-peaked mountain range. We flew higher still, soaring up the incline of the mountains, and then right over its ragged pinnacle.

Over the other side I could see a clear, turquoise ocean that looked motionless from this distance, and I could make out the dark shapes of coral reefs within its depths. The sun was brighter here, and so I gauged that we had been heading east.

How far away are we from other supernatural lands? Which race lives closest? I made a mental note to ask Ruby – no doubt Ash would have been more forthcoming about the exact location of Nevertide, if he even knew. The sentries seemed so closed off here – with or without the borders, and I wondered if this was a choice made by the kingdoms to cut themselves off from the dangers of the rest of the supernatural realm.

Soon the bird dropped lower, and I could see the forests and rocky beaches that surrounded the water. We swooped down, the tips of the vulture's wings almost brushing the leaves of the dense tree formations. Soon I saw a clearing in the forest, not far back from the water's edge, and the vulture landed on its soft white sand.

I slipped out of Tejus's grip and hastily climbed down from the creature. I looked around me, stunned into silence by the large, looming shapes that emerged from the ground.

It looked like a graveyard of ancient relics. I could see the top of what looked like a Viking longship. It was half submerged in the sand. Large, empty chests lay rotted and turned over, their contents long gone, but their Norse writing still clearly marked on the silver joints. Old and rusted weaponry lay wedged between driftwood, the round shields marked with Gaelic crosses and runes.

"This is… *incredible*," I managed to gasp out.

"Relics left over from the first sentries," Tejus commented.

"You mean Vikings?" I replied, picking up what was left of a rusty blade.

"Pardon?"

"Vikings," I repeated slowly, "all this is old Viking stuff."

Tejus looked at me as if I was speaking another language.

"Longship." I pointed at the boat. "Nordic chests, runes—all this is obviously from the Viking era—you know, the bloodthirsty invaders that ransacked all the villages?"

"I don't understand," he replied slowly.

"Don't you learn history here?" I asked, exasperated.

Tejus frowned at me. "This is from the first sentries," he said. "They were seafaring people, and were the first to discover Nevertide. They came from an ancient land now claimed by ocean, and settled here thousands of years ago."

I frowned in confusion. "But... this looks like one hundred percent *Viking* stuff. Vikings are from Earth. I studied them in depth, at school." I felt I was right, but it was confounding. If these were from Vikings, then had those Vikings come here and then... *become* sentries?

"Are you certain?" Tejus questioned me, not bothering to mask his deep curiosity.

"I'm quite sure," I replied, gazing around. "Is there a particular reason you brought me here, Tejus?"

He shrugged. "You showed me the place where you go to think... I just thought I would show you mine. Though I'm not sure if it will have quite the same effect in the future," he muttered, looking over at the longship.

I recalled our mind meld where I'd shown him the

beach near The Shade's Port. I couldn't help but feel a bit touched that he'd remembered and sought to do the same.

"Thanks. I, uh, appreciate it."

Suddenly feeling strangely self-conscious, I walked over to another relic lying in the sand that looked like some sort of bronze figurine.

The next moment, I was falling through the ground with my limbs flailing in all directions and landing with a very painful thump on a hard surface. I lay there for a moment or two in shock, and then groaned when my back jerked in agony.

"Hazel!" Tejus peered down at me from above.

"Yeah," I muttered, trying to sit up slowly.

"Don't move," he called. "I'm coming down."

"Don't do that—we might never get out," I replied, short-tempered due to the pain in my back.

Where am I?

The hole that I'd fallen through gave me just enough light to see through the gloom. At first I thought it was a sort of cave, hollowed out over time by the sea. But as I looked more closely at my surroundings, I could see inscriptions on the walls, which were definitely man-made. Standing up slowly, and walking to the nearest wall, I thought they were Viking symbols, but these looked different to what I'd seen on the chests and weaponry.

Then I realized the surface I'd landed on was a large stone monolith that stood in the center of the space. All around the block were the same carved inscriptions, their lines harsh and jagged as if they'd been created using very rudimentary tools.

Beyond the stone block, I could see a narrow passageway.

"Wait, I think there's another entrance," I called to Tejus. "I'm going to see if it will lead me out... It's so strange down here."

I ducked my head and began to creep silently along. The air felt stagnant, and had Tejus not been waiting above, I didn't know if I'd have had the courage to walk along the darkened passage. As it was, I felt an uneasy sense of dread as I stumbled along in the blackness.

After a few yards, the air smelt fresher and I could faintly hear the sound of waves in the distance. I quickened my pace, and eventually emerged into the forest.

"Tejus?" I called, looking around.

I heard the thrashing of bushes, and he appeared before me.

"Are you hurt?" he asked, looking me up and down.

"My back doesn't feel great, but it's okay. Let's go back

this way," I urged him, "I don't know *what* this place is, but it almost looks like some kind of weird temple."

Tejus practically had to crawl down the passageway, the ceiling was so low. When we entered the room, he straightened up again and stared around him in surprise.

"Do you recognize any of it?" I asked in a hushed whisper. There was something about the place, like a museum or gallery, that made me want to lower my voice so as not to disturb anything.

Tejus didn't answer me, but made his way over to one of the walls and ran his fingers down the engravings. He then turned back to the stone structure in the middle of the room and crouched down to get a better look.

For the first time, I noticed that the top of the block had a deep groove running around its surface, and then an opening at one end, like a basic drainage system. I took a step back.

"This looks like a *sacrificial* table," I murmured, kind of freaked out.

"I think you're right. I recognize some of these symbols..." He hesitated.

"What?"

"Well—it's just strange. The markings belong to an old cult, formed after the first dwellers arrived here. But I didn't think any of it remained, not in such pristine form. We have some old stone disks back at the castle, but they are far more worn and aged than what's here." He looked up to the hole I'd fallen though. "Perhaps the sand preserved it?" he mused to himself.

"What was the cult for?" I asked, looking everywhere but the sacrificial table.

"They worshiped an old entity—not a god as such, but a mystical being that they believed was a source of extreme power. There is one manuscript on the subject and it's not very illuminating. But the cult is long forgotten. This place wouldn't have been used in many lifetimes."

I looked around at the floor and the passageway.

"Are you sure about that?" I asked quietly.

"Of course. Why?"

"Tejus, there isn't a speck of dust other than from when I fell, and as you say, the place doesn't look aged at all. In fact it looks well kept."

Tejus looked around.

I'm right. Someone's been here recently. I know it.

It wasn't just the lack of dust. I could *sense* that it had been used—that people had been here only recently.

"You might be right," he replied eventually. He looked disturbed by the fact, the frown lines on his forehead deepening.

I felt the sudden urge to leave, and put as much distance between us and this strange cave as possible.

Julian

"What exactly are we looking for?" Yelena called out from the back of the line.

"I don't know exactly," I called back, "but we just need to keep going until we can *feel* the barrier, we'll know when we get there."

My plan was to find the barrier first, and then try to walk at least part of its circumference, looking for a potential break in the force field. We had exited through the front gates of the castle through the portcullis, and Jenney had bad-temperedly drawn a line on an old map as to where she thought the barrier lines might begin. It would take us most of the day to reach them, and we might be following the line around well into the night. We'd packed provisions, subtly, so the guards wouldn't realize we were out for the long haul, and each carried them in makeshift packs on our back.

"I still think this is a bit of a fool's errand," Benedict grumbled.

"If we find what we're looking for you'll be thanking me," was all I could think to say.

The line was making slow progress. I kept having to pause and wait for them to catch up to us. I'd only taken half of the kids with me, the more energetic of the bunch, but even then most of them seemed half asleep, dragging their feet along with their shoulders hunched.

"What is it with this lot anyway?" I asked Benedict. "Why aren't they getting any better? They all look half dead. They've had *days* to recover."

He shrugged noncommittally and I noticed that he didn't look much better. In the direct light, I could clearly make out the heavy bags under his eyes and the pallor of his skin.

Up ahead was a large forest, marked on the map as Devel Wood. It went on for miles, but after that there was just an open expanse of meadow which would lead us to where Jenney estimated the closest barrier line lay.

"Okay," I announced to the group. "In the forest, stick together. If you lose sight of Benedict or me, call out and we'll come and find you. Whatever you do, don't go wandering about on your own, okay?"

"What if we get lost?" one of the kids called out.

"You're not going to get lost," I explained patiently. "Just keep calling and we'll find you—hold hands if you want, but in pairs only."

The path started off easy, with the trees sparsely placed so that sunlight dappled down onto the forest floor and fallen leaves crunched underfoot. Up ahead was nothing but gloom—the trees were more densely populated and their huge boughs and branches blocked the sky. Unless we crossed it by sundown, we'd get completely lost in the dark.

I didn't want to share my concerns with Benedict—he was already being negative enough—but I felt a slight pang of regret that I'd insisted on taking the kids along with us. I didn't know what animals or creatures lay in the dark recesses of a Nevertide forest and Jenney had never ventured into them, so her knowledge was limited, but I dreaded coming across any of them. When a group of people kept vultures and bull-horses as transportation methods and pets, you could bet that whatever animals hid in the dark would be ten times worse.

But it was too late to turn back.

"I don't like this," Benedict whispered as we crossed over into the gloom of the thick trees. "There's something not right."

"Don't be silly," I replied a little hastily, "it's fine."

"No, it's not… Can't you hear that?"

I stopped still and listened for the slightest of sounds, but couldn't hear a thing.

"No."

"Exactly. How many times have you been in a forest when you couldn't hear the sound of a bird or something making a racket in the undergrowth?" he whispered.

Oh.

He was right. There was no sound coming from the forest—nothing. The silence suddenly felt oppressive, a thick blanket that suffocated us as we stood still, the blood rushing in my ears the only thing I could hear…

Then the howls began.

HAZEL

The next morning, I was woken abruptly by a loud banging coming from the door to Tejus's living quarters. I'd had a dreamless sleep, which was a relief, but it had taken me a long time to halt the flashing memories of the eerie cult temple and its sacrificial table before I was able to drop off.

I opened the door to my cubby hole as the banging continued, and crawled out to see Tejus striding across the room wearing nothing but a towel and still dripping wet from his bath.

My mouth went a tad dry.

I had seen Tejus bare before, during the nymph incident

in his father's labyrinth, and it wasn't an image I was likely to forget—but I wasn't going to lie, this morning's refresher was a welcome sight. I couldn't help but stare at the defined muscles of his back and shoulders as he pulled open the door with impatient force.

Distracted, I didn't pay much attention to our visitors until I could hear voices being raised. I hung back, uncertain about the nature of the argument, but soon I could hear my own name being mentioned and I approached the doorway—keeping a good distance between me and Tejus's bare torso.

"It is the rules," a guard replied heatedly. "Necessary for the trial. You have no jurisdiction over this, Prince."

There were three of them standing at the door, all dressed in their palace livery.

"On whose authority?" Tejus questioned.

"The ministers. Failure to comply will result in disqualification from the rest of the trials."

"What's going on?" I interrupted.

The guards turned to me as Tejus shot me a silencing glare, which I ignored.

"We need to escort you to the location of the next trial," replied one of the guards, "*without* your champion," he emphasized for Tejus's benefit.

"I won't allow it," Tejus bit out.

"One moment, please." I smiled at the guards and pushed the door partway shut.

"What are you doing?" I asked, turning on Tejus. "Do you want us to get disqualified from the trials? Jenus is banished from the kingdom, so it's not like he's a threat anymore… and I'm sure my *kidnapper* won't be bothering us again," I added sarcastically.

He gave me a quizzical look, but remained silent and stony-faced.

"I don't trust them," he muttered eventually.

"It doesn't look like we have a choice. Do I need to remind you that I have as much invested as you in the outcome of the trials? We can't say no, Tejus."

I crossed my arms, until he sighed. Before moving to reopen the door, he hesitated and turned toward me, taking my hands gently in his.

"Hazel, please stay safe. Be cautious…don't do anything reckless."

Where did that come from?

It almost sounded like Tejus had come to care for me – more than just as a prized possession to help him get through the trials. His touch was warm, and the expression on his face showed genuine concern and…tenderness? I couldn't be sure – but I felt a warm glow suffuse my body.

"Okay," I murmured. "I'll be careful. I promise."

He nodded, the corners of his mouth turning up ever so slightly into an almost smile. He removed his hands slowly, reluctantly.

Then the smile dropped from his face completely as he turned back toward the door, and the cold, indifferent mask returned.

"Fine." He called to the waiting guards. "Take her."

I dashed off to find robes and hastily dressed in the bathroom. I emerged a short while later and allowed the guards to escort me down to the castle courtyard. They were silent, and I didn't bother asking any questions—it seemed pointless when I knew they'd inevitably go unanswered.

Once we arrived at the courtyard, I was relieved to see other humans milling about—and Ruby's distinctive blonde hair.

"Hey," I said, walking over to her.

She smiled faintly as I approached, "Do you know what's going on here?" she asked.

"Not a clue. As per usual."

"I'm glad you're here," she replied. "I thought Tejus might not allow it... I noticed he didn't like you dancing with that other champion—what's his name?"

"Nikolay," I answered. "Yeah. I don't think Tejus is a fan…"

Before I could make a quip about her and Ash, our conversation was cut short as another one of the guards approached us—a different one to the men who had brought me down here.

"Hazel?" he queried. "You must come with me."

I looked past him to see a small bull-horse-drawn carriage marked by the distinctive livery of the Hellswan household—an image of a gold vulture's head marking the side of the door.

"We're not going together?" I asked, taking a step back.

"Each human has their own carriage," he replied.

Ruby and I had no choice but to part ways. I followed the guard back to the waiting carriage, waving goodbye to Ruby as I did so.

"Where are we going?" I asked as we reached the door.

"Well now, I can't tell you that," he replied, unexpectedly jovial, "but I can tell you that there's nothing to be afraid of—as far as you humans are concerned, this is the gentlest trial of the lot."

I nodded my thanks as he opened the door. I stepped into the carriage, admiring the plush velvet seats and the satin padding on the ceiling. The guard shut the door behind me, and I instantly peered out of the window to look for Ruby. I could see her, not far off, stepping into another carriage alone.

The bull-horse started to clop its hooves on the ground, and soon we were riding over the moat and along the main passageway that led past the forest and down to the villages. I soon realized why the ceiling was coated in fabric—the ride was a bumpy one, and I had to clutch onto the seat with both hands to avoid hitting my head as the wheels bounced over the cobblestones.

The villagers had come out to see what the procession was about—I guessed a formation of six carriages through the sleepy hamlet wasn't something they were necessarily used to. I waved at them as we went past, and they waved back, kids being placed on their parents' shoulders to get a better look at the humans, and staring as we drove by.

I started to feel like a museum exhibit. It was a relief when the houses trickled out of sight and were replaced with farmland, with a ginormous mountain range and more forests in the distance.

"How far have we got to go?" I called out to the guard from the open window.

"'Bout an hour or two... depending. You just get

comfy. There's bread and water under the seat if you get hungry," he replied.

I thanked him and continued staring out of the window, letting my mind relax in anticipation of the long journey. The ride was smoother here, and I let go of the seat, sinking comfortably back into the cushions. As I looked out over the flat plains of the meadows, the image of Tejus and his lack of attire this morning flickered briefly in my mind, and I hastily shoved it away.

Don't go back there, I warned myself.

Roughly an hour later, we started to enter the forest. There was a wide path cut through in the middle of it, and we trundled along, a few stray branches scratching at the body of the carriage. I realized that I hadn't heard the carriages behind for a while, and stuck my head out of the window to look. They were gone. We were alone.

"Where are the others?" I called out to the guard.

"Still awake, are you?" He smiled down at me. "They've gone someplace else. You'll see why later. Don't worry though—I know this place like the back of my hand. My ma was a hermit and lived on the other side of this place. Know all its tricks," he murmured, looking around at the looming trees and moss-covered rocks that lay on either side of the path. "Not much further to go now," he continued, "you just relax. We've got a bit of a walk ahead of us."

Once again I thanked him and lay back in the seat. But I couldn't relax. The forest was pleasant, with its dappled shade and sweet-smelling perfume of oak and aspen trees, but something about it made me uneasy and tense, as if there were eyes watching me from the undergrowth, creatures that hid from the light of day. I shuddered and resisted the urge to close my eyes—I didn't know what this trial would entail, but if for whatever reason I needed to get myself out of this forest, knowing the trail would work in my favor.

The trail started to incline, and we no longer went in a straight path, but seemed to be winding our way around the base of a mountain. The sheer drop below, on the right side of the carriage, became higher and higher at each twist and turn.

Eventually we reached a flatter section of the path, and it widened out onto a small grassland with narrow trails winding off up into the mountain.

"We stop here," the guard alerted me. "How are you feeling?"

"I'm fine," I replied shakily, stepping out onto the solid ground with relief.

"Good." He smiled as he jumped down from his bull-horse and retrieved some small black items from a sack by his seat. "Now comes the uncomfortable part. I'm going to need to blindfold you and tie your hands behind your back." He revealed the items to be a short piece of rope and a blindfold.

Are you kidding me?

"What!" I exclaimed. "No way!"

"Don't worry, nothing's going to happen," he tried to reassure me. "Look, now that we're here I can tell you the details of the trial. The aim of this game is for your champion to 'find' you using your mental bond, so your senses become a guide for them. What you smell and hear will alert them to your location—that is, if they know enough about the lay of the land, and are able to fully immerse themselves in your bond. A trick that few can manage, as I understand it, but you're with Tejus," he concluded merrily, "he'll have no problem."

I digested the information, horrified by the fact that I'd be stuck in a strange forest with my senses impaired. Once again it angered me that the trials appeared to be putting the humans in danger, just for the sport of the champions.

"So you'll just leave me alone... in the forest?" I confirmed.

"Oh, no. The prince would have my neck. I'll be a few paces off, keeping watch—you won't come to any harm."

That reassured me, but only slightly.

The guard started to bind my wrists together behind my back. The knot was tight, but not uncomfortable and I found that I could flex my wrists easily.

"Why do I need to be tied up, anyway?" I asked.

"So you can't cheat and remove your blindfold," he replied. "The ministers aren't really a trusting lot."

Next he tied on the blindfold—a thick piece of fabric that was densely woven so that nothing could be seen through it. He wrapped it around my head three times and then tied it securely at the back.

"How many fingers am I holding up?" he asked.

"I don't know," I muttered. *And I sure wouldn't tell you if I did.*

We continued upward, walking on what I assumed was one of the paths I'd seen leading from the grassland. The guard led me the entire time, his solid presence the only thing I had to guide and anchor me.

I didn't like it. I felt helpless and debilitated. Our journey was slow and frustrating—I was so wary of making a wrong move that I hesitated each time I took a step forward, leveraging my foot down slowly to check there was nothing but firm earth beneath me, even though the guard assured me I was safe.

I huffed, but didn't reply. Soon I felt the earth flatten out beneath me and become softer than the dry dirt we'd previously been walking on.

"We'll stop around here," he told me after a while. "I'm going to sit you up by a tree so you've got something to ground you. You can move around if you want, but be careful. There's a cliff edge not far off, so go slow."

Great. A cliff edge.

The guard helped me sink down next to the tree, and I felt the bark graze against my back.

"So, soon you'll feel Tejus reach out for you. Let your senses guide him so that he can find you," he instructed.

"But I feel sense-less!" I said. "How long is the trial expected to last?"

"As long as it takes until you're found."

I leaned glumly back against the tree.

"I'm going to back away from you now," the guard said.

I heard his heavy footsteps walk off into the distance, and eventually the shake of shrubbery and breaking of twigs as he found a place to wait, which I presumed to be further back in the forest.

I waited and waited, until finally, I began to feel the

familiar soft, feathery touches fluttering at my temples and inside my head.

Tejus.

I reached out to him as best I could, accepting the bond and trying to keep a steady hold of it. Which was difficult. We'd never attempted this at long range before, and it was almost like trying to get a crappy radio signal, with the frequency jumping in and out.

Not wanting to waste time, I tried to send him images of my recollections from the journey—the ride over the meadows and then into the forest. I felt him latch on to the forest image, and assumed that he clearly recognized it, but then the bond became agitated and I could feel his frustration—*where in the forest?*

That I didn't know exactly. I could only send him the last image that I'd seen, and the multiple pathways that had snaked off into the mountain.

The connection broke.

I strained my ears, but heard nothing but the fluttering of leaves in the breeze and the sporadic chirps of birdsong. I twisted my wrists in the bonds, wishing I could in some way feel the land around me. There was nothing I could touch but a few stones around the base of the tree...

The stone!

It was in the pocket of my robe. I was positive that it would help strengthen the connection—maybe give Tejus some access to my memory that would help him. The only problem was my hands.

Slowly I struggled into a standing position, and leant against the tree. The robe was a loose garment, and I thought that if I could twist it round enough, using the trunk of the tree, I'd probably be able to reach the pocket.

I ran the material across the bark, trying not to look too weird while I was doing it so as not to attract the attention of the guard. Eventually the fabric caught on the bark, and I dragged it round, grabbing on to its folds with my hands. It took a while, but eventually I was rewarded by the heavy clunk in my hands. My fingers fiddled with the fabric, trying to find the pocket opening.

Come on... come on...

I wanted to grab the stone before Tejus tapped back into my mind and saw what I was doing. Eventually my fingers touched the cold, smooth surface and I mentally gave myself a pat on the back.

I held the stone tightly.

Nothing happened for a few moments, and I panicked that even the stone wasn't going to be of any use in this ridiculous trial. As I waited for something to happen, I started to see dark shadows through the blindfold. At first I just thought it was my imagination getting bored of seeing nothing but black, but the shadows morphed into an image that became clearer and clearer by the second, as if I was seeing a photo negative held up to the light.

What the hell...

The images grew sharp. I could see the trees and the stone clusters in front of me, the long grass that surrounded the tree. I turned around, and saw the cliff edge about three yards ahead.

The stone has given me the sentry True Sight!

The realization was so shocking I almost dropped it from my hand.

As it was, I suddenly felt overwhelmed by its powers. I had always assumed it was an energy stone, not much different from the crystals that Tejus kept in his cubby hole, just more potent. I had *seriously* underestimated the kind of power that it had.

Pushing the thought to one side, and determined to make the most of its powers before Tejus connected again, I shuffled onto my knees and hobbled off toward the cliff edge. Once I was close enough, I lay on my stomach and peered over the edge.

Its drop seemed to go on for miles, and there was

nothing but an almost smooth drop of rock—except for the waterfall that cascaded through a crevice in the stone down to the left. I could just about hear it from here—the violent crashing waters cascading into a river off in the distance. This *must* be able to help.

I shuffled away from the cliff and placed the stone in the back pocket of the trousers I wore beneath my robe. I couldn't afford to still have it in my hands when Tejus found me.

I focused on trying to call Tejus back and grow the bond once more. After a few tries I found him and latched on, feeling his relief floating through the connection. I pictured the waterfall in my mind and sent it over to him, encapsulating as much of the image as I could recall. I felt the vision 'take' and then a burst of recognition and surprise flooding through our bond.

Satisfied, I let the connection go.

Now all I had to do was wait, and while I was doing that, come up with a good excuse as to how I'd seen the waterfall in the first place.

It didn't take long.

I heard the sound of a bull-horse cantering up the mountain, the boughs of trees whipping as it crashed through the undergrowth.

"Hazel!"

Tejus might have me on edge most of the time, but right now his voice was the thing I most wanted to hear in all the world.

"I'm here!" I cried out.

"Are you all right?" I heard him rushing toward me, and then he knelt down and took me roughly in his arms.

"I'm fine," I murmured, my voice muffled by his cloak. He ripped the blindfold off my face and looked into my eyes, his face barely an inch from mine.

He jerked away from me suddenly as the guard came forward from his hiding place.

"What were you thinking?" Tejus snapped at him, jumping to his feet. "Do you know how much danger she could have been in?"

The guard held out his arms in defense. "I was only following orders, Prince Tejus—rules of the trial and the ministers."

"He was kind," I interjected on the guard's behalf. "It's not his fault."

Every muscle in Tejus's body seemed to coil with tension.

"Leave. We'll be behind you," he commanded the guard

coldly. The guard nodded before he shot off down the path to his waiting carriage.

When he was gone, Tejus resumed his study of me – checking I was unharmed. He turned me around slowly, making sure I didn't lose my balance, gently pushing me to lean against his chest while he reached down and untied the bonds. When the rope fell to the ground, I flexed my wrists and cramped fingers. I felt Tejus's hands close over my lower arms, and he slowly, but firmly rubbed up and down, helping the blood rush back into my hands.

"I'm fine," I murmured, hearing his rapid heartbeat thump furiously against where my head lay resting. His closeness was making my throat constrict, my stomach lurched uncomfortably as I inhaled the muskiness of his scent and my frame felt completely eclipsed by his. Mouth dry, I took a step back – afraid that he would soon hear my heartbeat hammering like his, for no logical reason.

What is happening to me?

Just because my rescuer had come dashing through the forest to untie me, it did not mean that I should fall into the role of the panting damsel in distress. I really needed to get a hold on myself and reality, *now*.

"I don't know how you did it," he said with a curious expression, seemingly completely unaffected by our closeness. It helped reality assert itself. "How did you see the waterfall?"

"My blindfold slipped a bit when I crawled to the edge—obviously I didn't know it was a cliff edge," I bumbled, averting my eyes from the intensity of his gaze. He was silent for a moment, watching me.

"All right," he said slowly. I sensed he was suspicious, but he didn't ask me any further questions, which was a relief—I didn't know how long I would have stood up to his scrutiny.

He hoisted me up onto the bull-horse and then leapt on himself, placing himself in front of me.

"Hold on," he said, and then set off at a thundering pace down the mountain. I clung to the solid muscle of his waist and leaned my head against the folds of his robes. I closed my eyes, preferring not to see the side of the cliff face dropping below us or the trees rushing past us in a green blur.

In half the time that it had taken me to get there, I was back in the castle courtyard. A bunch of ministers and red robes observed with their jaws hanging open. There was no crowd yet—everyone must have presumed that the trial wouldn't be ending for hours.

We did it too soon!

I realized that in my haste to get out of there, I had put us under suspicion. It didn't matter what the ministers thought—they were overjoyed that Tejus had gained yet another twenty points, putting him on par with Ash for the time being. If Ash also succeeded in this trial, he would gain ten points and remain slightly ahead—but as there were only two more trials to go, the competition between the two would now be a very close call.

When the congratulations from the ministers died down, Tejus took me aside.

"We need to go back inside," he said.

"I want to see if Ruby and Ash make it," I said. "I'm worried about Ruby—it's going to get dark soon."

"Fine. You can watch from the tower."

That worked for me. I didn't particularly relish the thought of waiting around for hours surrounded by ministers.

After a quick bath, I wrapped myself in a thick blanket and I went up to the tower. Tejus joined me, sitting on the other side of the turret, his eyes off in the distance—apparently unconcerned with who returned now that he'd succeeded in winning the trial.

It was just after dusk when Ash and Ruby arrived. There was a crowd gathered below now, and they'd lit bonfires and torches across the grounds to greet the champions. I smiled to myself as she disembarked from Ash's bull-horse, and they raised their arms to greet the waiting crowd.

A figure walked up to them and tapped Ruby on the shoulder. She turned round to greet the stranger, and after a few moments they walked together over to the nearest bonfire. In the light I could make out the unmistakable blue robes and pronounced features of Queen Trina Seraq.

Well... that's strange...

What could they possibly be talking about?

BEИEⓄICТ

Jenney had covered all our cuts and bruises with a thick, nasty-smelling paste that hadn't really improved my mood. Not only did my entire body ache, but now I smelt like some kind of disgusting herb.

No one spoke at the breakfast table, but there were some dark mutterings coming from some of the older kids, and I had a sneaky suspicion that there was a revolt afoot within the Hell Raker ranks regarding leadership. Julian was not popular right now—our mission had been a total and dismal failure.

As soon as we'd heard the eerie sounds of howls echoing through the forest, we'd all turned and run. I didn't want to wait around to see what bloodthirsty creatures waited for us in the undergrowth—we'd faced enough danger since we'd entered Nevertide. We'd only stopped when we reached the castle walls, and then, panting—and with some of the younger kids crying—we'd all returned to our living quarters. Jenney hadn't said anything, just pointedly sighed in Julian's direction and muttered something about 'impatience' as she tended our wounds.

In the short time that we'd been gone, new recruits had arrived. There were three, one girl and two boys. As they tucked into their breakfast with enthusiasm, I couldn't help but notice how much *healthier* they looked than the rest of us. One of the new boys, Dean, was seated between Yelena and another kid who had been with us from the start. I couldn't understand why they looked so drawn and pale, listlessly prodding their food, while he looked the picture of health—hadn't his mind been drained to exhaustion by the sentries? And why did all the other kids who'd been here longer look so crappy? I looked over at Julian. He didn't look much better than the rest of them.

As far as I was aware, I was the only one having trouble sleeping and experiencing weird dreams—none of the others had complained of anything, not that I'd heard anyway.

"I hate that we turned and ran like cowards," Julian muttered from the end of the table. We all looked at him, but no one said anything.

"We didn't have much choice," I answered eventually.

"Some vigilante group we are, giving up at the first hurdle!" he retorted. "We're supposed to be taking action, getting out of here on our own and not waiting around for some sentry to decide when we can leave."

"You were trying to get through the barriers on your own?" Dean, the new boy, asked in disbelief.

"Yeah, why?" Julian looked at the other boy across the table.

"Nothing." He shrugged. "It's just that I've heard it's impossible—my sentry told me that the barriers are erected by all the minister sentries using their collective mind power. I don't think there's going to be a way through till they lower them after the trials. Sorry, man."

"I'm not giving up," Julian replied stubbornly.

"You probably should," I replied. "We're wasting our time. We have to just wait it out—there's only two more trials to go. I don't think anything's going to happen to us in that time, and both Ash *and* Tejus have the highest scores."

Julian flung his spoon down and looked at me with

disappointment. I thought he was going to say something, but instead he pushed his chair back and left the room.

I stared at my plate, not wanting to see the looks the kids were giving me. I didn't understand why Julian had to be so pig-headed about this. But I couldn't deny that I was also a bit worried that I didn't seem to *care* that much about escaping Nevertide. The Shade had started to feel like such a far-away place... It was weird.

"Are you okay?" Yelena asked softly.

"I'm fine," I muttered, my jaw tightening.

"Well, I'm going to go and do something with Julian— you know, like sword train—so he feels like we're at least doing *something*."

Be my guest.

She stood up to leave, and out of the corner of my eye I saw other kids doing the same.

"Come with us, Benedict," one of them called, "you're really good at it."

"Yeah, come on!" another one chorused.

I sighed inwardly and followed them.

We all made our way over to the weapons hole we'd created under a loose stone in the floor and armed ourselves with the rusty, ancient relics.

"These are so *cool!*" Dean exclaimed, and it made me

feel marginally better.

By the time we'd entered the deserted courtyard we were using as our practice yard, I was in a better mood and started to parry with Dean, letting Julian take over the instruction of the younger kids.

We had only been there ten minutes when a small cry came from Yelena. I turned around to see one of the youngest girls had fallen to the floor in a faint. Dropping my sword with a clatter on the floor, I rushed over to the girl.

She lay white-faced and breathing ever so softly, while I stood over her body, panicked and anxious.

There was something familiar about the scene that lay before me.

The limp body reminded me of Yelena as she'd lain fast asleep in the living quarters, with me standing over her, my arms outstretched.

I felt a strange, sick feeling in the pit of my stomach.

There was something that I was meant to understand about all this—a half-thought forming in my mind. I recalled the pale, drawn faces around the table. My midnight wanderings around the castle. And the stone. Always the stone...

Was *I* responsible, somehow, for this strange lethargy

that had taken us all?

But that was impossible...

Wasn't it?

HAZEL

Tejus had offered to show me around the grounds of the castle—there were so many parts that I still hadn't seen, especially outside. Even so, I had agreed reluctantly. I felt that it was a premeditated maneuver on his part to start talking about what happened with the waterfall and the blindfold. Since that afternoon, I had caught him glancing at me occasionally, with a curious, questioning expression on his face. He knew my lie didn't add up—and I couldn't think of another way to explain it without revealing the truth.

We entered a small courtyard that I'd not seen before, with a dried-up water fountain in the middle which contained dried leaf debris. The wind was cold that morning, and it whipped unkindly around the stone walls of the courtyard, sounding hollow and bleak.

"I wanted to congratulate you, Hazel." Tejus spoke first, and I looked up at him as he gestured for me to take a seat on the edge of the fountain. I complied, finding the ice-cold marble uncomfortable.

"You seem to be able to see so much," he continued, and my heart sank. "In my mind, I mean. Our ability to connect is something I've never come across before... It far surpasses any expectations I had. Even when I try to block you out, you seem to be able to find a way in. It's... remarkable."

"When did you try to block me out?" I asked, trying to change the subject so I wouldn't have to take credit where it wasn't due. I felt guilty. His praise wasn't deserved—it was all the damn stone.

"At the beginning of the honest trial. It was overwhelming... I felt *weak*," he replied hesitantly. "People should never see me that way. For obvious reasons."

"Maybe if you were to show your people vulnerabilities, they might like you more," I replied cautiously.

"I don't want them to like me. They need a leader," he

responded curtly. "They might like the story of a kitchen boy rising to kingship, but what the people of Nevertide need is someone to rule them—someone who knows the politics of the kingdoms."

"Maybe." I shrugged, wondering if Ash would have actually come first in a few of the trials if I hadn't used the stone. I no longer knew what skills Tejus actually had, and what was the work of the stone.

I wanted us to win the trials, but was I robbing the people of Nevertide of their rightful leader?

"Maybe?" Tejus repeated.

"Well… I suppose I don't know, do I?" I said. "Maybe you'd both be good at the job."

"It's reassuring to know you have such faith in me," he replied sarcastically.

I huffed and then we sat in silence for a while. Tejus stared ahead at the arched entrance, and I stared at my hands, mulling in a mixture of guilt and annoyance.

"You are behaving oddly," he finally declared.

I didn't dare meet his eyes. "Why do you say that?"

"You know that you are. What is the matter?" he asked.

His eyes bored into me, and I could sense the determination in them to get to the bottom of whatever was troubling me.

"I'm just homesick," I replied.

He nodded slowly, but I could tell he wasn't satisfied by my reply. I supposed homesickness wasn't something that Tejus would have ever understood. It wasn't like he would have anything much to miss here.

"Then... Why don't you share some of your human experiences with me? I'd like to see them again." I wasn't sure if this was a sincere request, or some kind of ruse. I looked at him suspiciously. His face was quite stony, as was its default state, but I couldn't deny there was a hint of real curiosity in his eyes.

Crap.

I needed to be careful when I shared my memories with Tejus. I didn't want him to know anything about The Shade or GASP members. I didn't think I'd ever trust *anyone* in Nevertide with that kind of information... And I didn't want the stone coming up either.

The only way around it would be to carefully pick a memory from one short vacation we'd gone on with our parents in Hawaii. I desperately wished I could use the stone in this moment—it would help me focus on what I wanted Tejus to see, without other thoughts drifting in, but I didn't dare risk it.

"Okay," I replied, preparing a memory.

I felt the familiar sensations at my temple and skull, and reached out to him as best I could. I felt the bond click into place, and then started to flesh out the memory as best I could for him.

We were at an open-air concert. We had managed to get last-minute tickets to see a band play. The sky had been lit by a million stars, and combined with the flashing stage lights and the stunning set design, the experience had been quite unreal.

I flicked through the images of that night for Tejus's benefit—the band on stage, and the lead guitarist crowd-surfing across the hysterical audience. How I had danced to every song, dripping with sweat by the end of it, but deliriously happy. A snapshot of Benedict playing air-guitar and looking like a total idiot.

Another image flickered into my mind—still at the concert, but if I remembered correctly, during one of the breaks. We were all leaning against the rail of the main dance floor.

"Hey, Hazel, can I have some money for a soda? I'm so thirsty," Benedict said.

I had been looking after his spending money in my pocket alongside my own.

I fumbled around in my jean pocket for his bag of

change, and, grabbing what I could, I held out my hand to Benedict.

Nestling in with the dimes and single-dollar notes was the stone.

What the hell...

I felt the ground start to jerk under my feet and the stars in the sky rushed toward me.

Then I looked at Benedict and screamed.

His face had become grotesquely distorted, his eyes black like a bare skull's and his jaw hanging unnaturally low. His hand reached out for the stone...

The connection broke.

I gasped, jerking violently away from the fountain as I fought for breath.

"What the HELL was that?" Tejus bellowed at me, his face cast in an expression of pure fury.

"I don't... I don't know!"

"Don't lie to me! What was that stone?" he hissed. He grabbed my hands, yanking me toward him, his face an inch from mine. "That thing had power—what the hell was it? Tell me, Hazel. Tell me *now.*"

"I'm... so, so sorry... I found it in the sword," I whispered.

"The sword of Hellswan?" he asked, his face blanching.

"Yes, it was in the handle."

"Damn it!" he swore. He dropped my arms in disgust and leapt up, starting to pace back and forth in front of me, clenching his fists as he did so. "We could have been disqualified if anyone had found it, do you realize that?" He spat out his words with such venom that I took a hasty step back.

"That stone has obvious powers," he continued, "I could feel it through the vision—and you should never trust *anything* that once belonged to my father. Why didn't you tell me?"

"I'm sorry. It was just so helpful…" I replied, feeling sick.

"I should have known." He glared at me. "A human would never possess such strong mental control. Such impressive abilities. You had me well and truly fooled! I thought it was all you—that you were something *special*."

He laughed bitterly.

His words cut sharply, brutally.

Don't cry, I scolded myself, feeling hot tears brim at the corners of my eyes, *don't let him see you cry*.

"I want you to take the stone and put it in the crystal room until I decide how to get rid of it without anyone seeing—or sensing its power. And don't you dare disobey me."

"I won't!" I shouted back at him. "It was a mistake—okay? And I said I was sorry!"

"Sorry doesn't help. You put everything at risk. Your own sibling's and friends' freedom—and my rightful place as the Hellswan ruler."

He might as well have just punched me in the gut for the effect his words had.

"I'm not listening to this anymore," I replied, my voice thick and hoarse. "I said I was sorry. I meant it. I'll put the stupid stone in the room—no one will ever know."

"Make sure you do," he growled.

He turned to walk away from me, but stopped when we both heard footsteps approaching.

"Hazel! I found you!" A voice echoed through the desolate courtyard. It was Nikolay, striding through the arch with a huge smile on his face and a bouquet of flowers in his hand.

"Oh, gods," Tejus muttered. He stalked off, walking past Nikolay without so much as a glance in his direction.

Nikolay watched him go with a look of bemusement on his face.

"Did I say something?" he quipped, winking at me and holding out the bouquet.

"No—I'm afraid that's all me," I replied, watching the departing figure.

"Are you okay?" he asked, peering down at me in concern.

"Yeah… I've just been a massive idiot," I replied bleakly.

"I don't believe that for a second. You are no idiot." He took my hand gently in his and raised the back of it to his lips. "You are a beautiful creature, Hazel—more angel than human, as I see it."

"That's very nice of you." I smiled back weakly, not exactly in the right frame of mind to enjoy Nikolay's flowery attentions. "But I *have* behaved like an idiot. It's something I need to go and fix."

I took my hand back, and his smile faded.

"Nikolay, it's not a good time." I turned to leave, but he stopped me.

"These still belong to you." He offered me the bouquet again and I took it before he continued. "Perhaps after the trials I can spend a bit more time with you?" he asked, less sure of himself now.

"Thank you for the flowers."

"There was nothing I could find that compared to your beauty," he called to me.

Seriously?

I waved at him, an artificial smile plastered across my face.

After I'd re-entered the castle and traipsed back upstairs to Tejus's living quarters, a disturbing realization surfaced in my mind, a realization that I could no longer deny.

The knightly charms of Nikolay all but repelled me. It was the cold, stony and occasionally cruel Tejus who—for reasons I couldn't fathom—I had begun to feel drawn to, even in spite of myself.

There is something seriously wrong with you, Hazel Achilles.

BENEDICT

I could hear the rustling of dry leaves outside my window, the dead ones scattering across the stone courtyards like rattling bones. The wind whistling through the castle seemed to whisper to me, calling out my name, urging me to get up.

Please don't call me again.

My mind whimpered, locked and helpless as my body rose in its state of half sleep. I passed Julian, lost to the world and snoring lightly into his pillow, and I longed to swap places with him, to sleep safely, unafraid of the corridors and hallways of the castle, a stranger to the call of the stone.

I passed the sleeping guards, quietly shutting the door behind me. The torches were still lit, throwing shadows across the walls.

My feet padded along the hallway, drawn further and further along into the shadows and the silence of the sleeping castle.

The whispers grew louder, more insistent. I needed to reach them, to find the voices that called out to me, to listen to the stones.

I came to a wooden doorway that I'd seen before, the one that Ash had led us through the day we returned to the castle in his sun-root cart.

Don't make me go outside! Please!

But the whispers kept calling.

My feet were bare, the cold stone like ice against my skin. I walked to the portcullis, its iron bars gleaming in the moonlight, the pointed tips like jagged teeth welcoming me into the dark beyond the castle walls.

Mindlessly I crawled onto the floor. There was a foot of space between the spikes and the floor, enough for me to crawl through. I inched my way beneath it, imagining that the iron frame would suddenly drop lower, claiming its victim, but I was unable to turn back. My body wasn't listening any more.

When I passed through, I raised myself upright again and walked along the moat. A bird's cry pierced the air. My blood ran cold, and I looked to the night sky, seeing a dark shadow briefly blocking out the moonlight. Soon I could hear the whoosh of wings growing closer, and a black vulture landed before me, fixing me with its beady glare, its gleaming coat of feathers looking like they'd been drenched in black tar.

Showing no sign of fear, just mindless acceptance of the whispered commands, I reached out for the bird. Holding on to a clump of feathers in my hand, I lifted myself onto the creature's back. Without a moment of hesitation, the bird soared through the air and carried me across the shadowed landscape of Hellswan.

I shut my eyes, my body intent on holding onto the vulture, my mind begging to be left to slide off its back and fall to the ground miles below.

Soon the bird dipped lower, and I could hear the violent crashing of the sea against rock. We almost skimmed the surface of its black waters—waters that looked to me to be endless, but when the bird came to a stop I found myself climbing down onto damp sand.

I looked around a forest clearing, lit only by a horrible green light that seemed to come from the sand itself.

Shapes rose up from the ground—boats, old chests, and the glint of battered weaponry. I walked past all these, drawn forward to a place where the light was the strongest, and found a large hole in the ground.

Don't look down, oh, God, don't look down…

The green light grew stronger—as if it had lit up the entire sky and the whole world in its sick, glowing green. I felt my legs trembling, so exhausted by the adrenaline that they started to give way. The whispers became screams, and they rocketed around in my head, filling it with white noise.

Then everything went black.

* * *

I came to groggily and looked around.

Where am I this time?

Dimly I could recall a green light and a hole in the ground, but as I looked around the sandy cove where I'd decided to make my bed for the night, there was nothing like that to be seen.

What I *could* see made me sit up in astonishment. I rubbed my eyes, unsure if I was really looking at a half-submerged Viking longboat rising out of the sand.

"You're awake." A female voice addressed me from

behind.

I shifted around hastily, and saw a blue-robed woman I'd seen at the trials smiling down at me.

"Wh-Who are you, and how did I get here?" I asked.

"I'm Queen Trina Seraq, and I don't know how you got here." She raised an eyebrow. "But you certainly gave me a shock."

"I'm sorry," I muttered, not sure what I was apologizing for.

"You're the brother of Tejus's human, aren't you?" she asked.

"Her name's Hazel," I replied coldly. "Yes, I am."

"I'm sorry." She smirked. "*Hazel*, of course. But what are you doing out here—so far from the protection of the castle?"

"I came with a…" I looked around, blankly.

How did I get here?

Queen Trina noticed my pause. "I can take you back—if you'd like? I have a carriage here; it wouldn't be any trouble."

"Okay… thanks."

"You can entertain me with the story of how you got here on our journey back." She smiled again, and I noticed how bright and sparkly her eyes were, as if she were laughing at some secret joke.

"It's hard to remember," I muttered, "but I keep sleepwalking, ending up in weird places, and I'm sure I've been walking about the castle at night… but this is the first time I've woken up outside."

I didn't know why I was opening up to her after keeping it a secret from Julian and the rest of them, but there was something about her that made me want to finally get some of the weirdness off my chest. Perhaps it was her curious manner, or the way she placed her arm over my shoulders, almost protectively, as we made our way to her carriage. Whatever it was about her, it was a relief to talk to *someone.*

Her carriage was small and black, raised on high wheels with a sleek, white bull-horse pulling at the reins. She had a driver too, a sentry in a navy-blue cloak that matched hers, but he didn't acknowledge us as we approached, just kept his eyes fixed on the road, waiting for Queen Trina's command.

The interior was made up of pinks, golds and blues, with countless cushions and sapphire crystals that hung over the windows so that the outside world looked like it was bathed in blue.

"Why don't you tell me when it started?" she asked

kindly as soon as we'd taken our seats and the bull-horse had started to trundle forward.

I told her everything. From the moment I'd found the wall of stones in the deserted and narrow corridor, to the moment she'd found me lying on the sand. I even mentioned the kids and how lethargic they had looked, and how I was afraid that it somehow had something to do with me.

"Don't be preposterous!" She laughed gently. "I think your imagination is getting the better of you, young man. It sounds to me like a great power is calling to you. Rather than see this as something scary, why don't you consider yourself honored? You have clearly been chosen to fulfil some great duty—your destiny, perhaps. Do you believe in destiny, Benedict?"

"Uh, I don't know," I replied.

"I do," she replied with a smile. "I believe that some of us are chosen for greatness—to accomplish incredible things with our lives, to shine a little more brightly than the others. I think *you* are going to shine," she whispered in my ear.

I didn't know about that.

It was true that this weird power had called only me so far as I knew, but I thought it was coincidence that had made me stumble on the wall of stones. I told the queen what I thought, but she gave me a pitying smile, as if there was something huge that I wasn't understanding.

"Power and greatness favor those who are brave, the adventurers. I don't believe that it was an accident. I think you are capable of far more than you understand at this moment—far more than you give yourself credit for. The worst thing you could do now," Queen Trina continued, "is to turn your back on this great power. Allow yourself to trust it, wave aside your old instincts, and embrace what the voices are telling you. Next time, Benedict, *pick up that stone.*"

I pursed my lips, doubtful. I wasn't sure what to think anymore.

"We're here," she said, the earnestness and seriousness gone from her tone. "It was lovely meeting you, Benedict. If you ever wish to visit, I'm staying in one of the old palaces near the Hellswan border —send a letter via guard and I will send you my personal vulture."

The carriage came to a halt, and her driver opened the door for me to get out. I managed an uncertain smile at Queen Trina as I left—my mind slightly blown away by the offer of a queen's personal transport. I'd never met a sentry so accommodating, one who hadn't tried to enter my mind *once*.

I crossed the moat with my head held higher and my back straighter.

Apparently, my destiny was waiting.

RUBY

When Queen Trina had pulled me aside last night and told me about the impending trial, my first instinct had been to try to work out what her motive could possibly be in wanting Ash to win the kingship. Or, more likely, what she stood to lose if Tejus won the trials.

To be fair, it hadn't been a great deal of information. She had claimed that the trial would be about testing the integrity of each champion, and that all would not be what it seemed.

No surprise there. There hadn't been a trial yet where I hadn't been taken aback by the powers of the sentries, nor the willingness of the ministers to go to any lengths to test them.

I paced back and forth across the small space of my bedroom, having firmly locked the door—the only time I could get privacy in our living quarters. I'd already shared the information with Ash, who had been equally perturbed about the source of the information, but had eventually shrugged, murmuring something about not looking a gift horse in the mouth.

My second concern was whether or not I should pass on the information to Hazel.

On one hand, we had decided to spread our bets—to align with different teams to ensure that one way or another, we got out of here. We had both agreed to pledge our mental energy to our chosen sentries, and so there was an element of competition whether we liked it or not, even if we were ultimately working toward one goal.

On the other hand, we were both children of The Shade. We were like family. Nothing should ever divide us—and we didn't betray one another to reach our own selfish goals.

If this was a trial of integrity, then I should show some.

I marched into the main living quarters, finding Julian slumped on the sofa looking listlessly into space.

"Where's Benedict?" I asked.

He shrugged. "I think he's off in the kitchens somewhere… I haven't seen him since this morning."

"Find him," I replied. "I don't like either of you wandering the castle by yourselves. I'm going to speak to Hazel. I won't be long."

He nodded, remaining seated on the sofa.

"Julian—*now*."

"I'm going, I'm going," he muttered. He rose from the sofa, and then hesitated.

"Ruby, there's something I need to…"

"What?" I replied impatiently.

"It's nothing." He shook his head. "Ignore me."

What is with everyone?

I guessed the kids must have started to get bored cooped up in the castle—the whole bunch of them were so lethargic and sleepy-eyed. And even Julian was acting weirder than normal.

Assuming Hazel would be in Tejus's quarters, I started to make my way to the staircase that led to his domain. I hoped he wouldn't be around. I wanted to have a private conversation with Hazel. Things had felt a bit weird between the two of us lately, and I hoped that this would put a stop to any underlying tensions.

Stepping out into the lobby of the stairwell, I heard

footsteps clattering down. Tejus was descending the staircase, his face grim.

"Hi, Tejus… Is Hazel upstairs?" I asked politely.

"Yes," he replied curtly. "Don't stay too long. She needs her rest."

She's not a child, I wanted to retort, but I kept my mouth shut. It wasn't in any of our interests to aggravate Tejus.

"Thanks," I replied, only a little sarcastically.

He didn't even seem to hear me, and marched past without so much as a nod in my direction.

What's eating him?

I carried on up the stairs and knocked on the door to his living quarters, ignoring the guards who stood on either side.

"Hazel?" I called.

The door swung wide open moments later.

Hazel appeared, looking tense, but her expression loosened as she laid eyes on me.

"Hi, Ruby."

"I saw Tejus on the way up," I said. "Is he always that grumpy?"

"Only on days ending with 'y'," she muttered.

We made ourselves comfortable on the sofas, sitting opposite one another with our feet up on the coffee table.

Had it not been for the medieval décor, we could have been back in The Shade on a lazy Sunday afternoon. It was nice. It had been too long since we'd just sat down, the two of us, without Benedict and Julian or looming sentries by our sides.

"How are you holding up?" I asked.

"I'm okay, you know… as okay as someone can be stuck in an alternate dimension having their mind sucked on a regular basis."

"At least Jenus is gone," I said. "I like spending time with Ash, and the boys seem to be coping."

"I haven't seen much of Benedict," Hazel replied. "I know it's my own fault—I'm spending too much time focused on the trials, and though I know it's for a good cause, I kind of feel like I'm being a lousy sister."

"Don't," I replied. "You just have to focus."

Hazel let out a breath, her eyes wandering the room worriedly before returning to me. "Well, you've never come up here before… what's the occasion?"

"Queen Trina Seraq," I said. "She shared some information with me last night about the next trial that I thought was only fair to share with you."

"Does Ash know you're telling me?" Hazel asked.

"What does that matter?" I was confused by the

question.

"Nothing," she amended hastily. "Sorry, go on."

I told her what the queen had told me, and watched as she digested the information.

"Not a lot to go on, is it?" she replied eventually.

I bristled a bit. It might not have been much, but at least it was *something*.

"No, I know that, but it's better than not knowing," I replied.

"I guess that's why Ash didn't mind you sharing the information," she replied. "I guess it doesn't give either of them much of an advantage."

"No, maybe not, but actually Ash *doesn't* know I'm telling you. I'll let him know later what I've done, but I don't need his permission to share something with my best friend!"

I realized I was getting defensive of Ash. It was just that he'd proven himself to be far more trustworthy than Tejus, in my opinion. At least *he* wasn't the one who'd kidnapped us in the first place.

Hazel looked contrite.

"Okay, Ruby. Thanks," she replied softly. Her voice was tinged with sadness, and I couldn't quite understand why.

"And you never know," I went on, even as I frowned at

her, "it might mean something to Tejus. Maybe he'll know something about how the ministers interpret integrity."

"You think the ministers know *anything* about integrity?" she deadpanned.

I couldn't argue with that.

"Did the *queen* let you know when the trial would be taking place?" Hazel asked, sneering at the word 'queen'.

"Nope… What have you got against Queen Trina?" I replied.

"Nothing, I guess… It's just that I found out she and Tejus used to have a *thing*."

"A romantic thing?" I was quite dumbfounded. Neither of them seemed capable of something like that—what did they do as hobbies, glower at each other?

"Apparently. I overheard them arguing about it—I think that's why Queen Trina tipped you off. She's determined for Tejus not to win. She denied that it was anything to do with their past, but it seems like her only possible motive."

I nodded. Well, this cleared *that* mystery up. Nevertide politics were more complicated than I'd originally thought.

We chatted for a bit longer, and though I tried as hard as I could, I couldn't quite break Hazel out of her gloomy mood—a mood that I felt I'd caused by telling her about the integrity trial. Maybe it was something to do with Queen Trina and Tejus, or maybe it was just my imagination, but whatever it was I couldn't get it out of her—and I left the room an hour later feeling more distant from Hazel than I ever had before. It wasn't a good feeling.

HAZEL

The next morning, I was up and dressed at the crack of dawn. I felt anxious and irritable—and guilty about keeping the stone a secret from Ruby. Part of me wanted to just run downstairs and tell her everything, no matter how she might respond to the news, but it also seemed pointless now. Tejus had forbidden me from using it at the next trial, and their scores were so close that it hardly mattered. One of the two was bound to win.

To make matters worse, I'd barely seen Tejus since our argument yesterday. He'd briefly come upstairs to check that the stone was in the crystal cubby-hole, and then left again without saying a word to me. I wanted to mend the situation before we were called to the next trial—being furious with one another wasn't going to help us achieve anything.

A moment later, the door swung open to the living room and Tejus swept through.

"The next trial will begin shortly. Are you ready?" he asked, merely glancing in my direction and then walking over to his wall to collect the Hellswan sword.

"Yes, I'm ready. Ruby visited me yesterday—"

"I don't care," he interrupted curtly. "We have a job to do, and I'm not interested in castle gossip."

What?

"It's a damn *game*, not a job—and it's not gossip—I have information about the trial!"

I realized that I'd made him mad by lying to him, but he had lied to me too about his relationship with the queen…he just didn't know I knew. But regardless of our secrets, we were still a team and I deserved more respect for helping us get this far.

"What is it then?" he replied.

"The trial is about testing your integrity—whatever that means *here*—and apparently not all will be what it seems. It's not a lot, I know," I added defensively when he raised his eyebrows, "but Queen Trina passed on the information to Ruby and Ash. I thought you should know."

His expression darkened.

"Come on, we need to leave," he said, clearly not willing to discuss the matter of Queen Trina. It seemed that whenever her name came up, Tejus shut down. During my eavesdropping I had overheard him saying that their parting had been difficult for him too—I wondered if it was still hard. If he still missed her, despite all she'd done to affect the outcome of the trials.

As we descended the staircase, Tejus spoke again.

"The trials are taking place on the Ghoul's Ridge," he informed me. "We will ride there together."

"*Ghoul's Ridge?*" That sounded kind of horrifying.

"It's just a name, Hazel. The land there is quite beautiful."

Wherever there was beauty in Nevertide, it wasn't long before something evil and dark was revealed on the flip side. I thought of the Viking cove, and shuddered at the memory of the sacrificial table and the eerie temple.

As we entered the courtyard, a guard brought Tejus's bull-horse forward and he briskly lifted me up in the saddle. Like last time, he jumped on in front of me and took the reins.

"Hold on, the ride is tricky," he instructed, barely

giving me enough time to do as he'd asked before he stuck his heels into the flanks of the bull-horse and we galloped off across the moat.

The ride was tiring. We were going at such a speed that I was forced to clutch on to Tejus and clench my thighs tightly around the horse so I wasn't bounced around on the saddle. Soon my entire body ached, and I longed to stand on solid ground again.

"It's up there," Tejus called to me, pointing out a large mountain range that I'd been able to see from his tower. It was so high that its peaks were almost completely obscured by clouds.

"Are we going right to the top?" I asked in alarm.

"Right to the top," he replied.

Great.

An hour or so later, the bull-horse was panting almost as much as Tejus as we broke through the cloud cover that had settled over the mountain and arrived at a sun-filled peak that traversed a long narrow ridge to an even taller summit ahead.

"Why do they call it Ghoul's Ridge?" I dared to ask once I was standing upright on the ground.

"It was a name given to it by farmers who used to use this mountain as grazing ground for their cattle. The winds blow strongly up here during certain seasons. This track"—his finger mapped out the narrow, yet flat-topped, causeway between the peaks—"was the reason many farmers failed to return to their homes. One strong gust of wind at the wrong moment and the hapless sentries would be sent flying off into oblivion."

Gulping, I took a few steps forward to see what lay on either side of the causeway. There was nothing but a sheer drop below, so deep that its end was invisible—blanketed by thick, swirling mists.

"Ghoul's potion," Tejus remarked.

"What?" I'd been so preoccupied by the view, I hadn't heard him approach.

"It's the name of the mists down there," he replied, staring down into its depths.

We continued onward and were the first to arrive at the ridge. I couldn't see any signs of the ministers or red robes yet and wondered how many of Ash's cheering committee would be here today, considering the geographical difficulties of the location.

It wasn't long before I found out. Finding a grassy knoll that faced the sun, I sat down to wait, wishing that Nevertide had sunscreen lotion and hoping that my pale skin wouldn't be fried to a crisp.

Eventually the ministers and red robes arrived, all on bull-horses, and behind them I saw the other two champions approaching: Ash, with Ruby behind him, and Nikolay with his human.

I rose to wave at them, and Tejus instantly appeared at my side.

"I trust you don't have the stone on you," he warned quietly.

"Of course I don't," I hissed back.

"Good."

He remained standing next to me, his arms folded, gazing stonily at the approaching champions. I turned away from him and, avoiding Nikolay, headed toward Ruby. We stood watching as the crowds rolled up the hill, some clearly having walked most of the way. The turnout was much larger than I'd expected, and I overheard a few of the ministers grumbling about it behind us. I idly wondered if that was why the trials were taking place here—had they wanted to reduce the crowd?

Queen Trina arrived with her personal entourage, and they set about building a small dais for her precious royal backside to be seated on.

"Sentries! Welcome!" the minister of ceremony addressed the crowd. I slowly made my way back to Tejus, and stood to listen by his side.

"Only three champions remain for the penultimate kingship trial. The test today will measure each champion's integrity—a vital and rare quality, but paramount to rulers of Nevertide. Champions, remember this—integrity will be measured by who can succeed, without *losing one's sense of self.*" He paused for dramatic effect, and then continued. "Ahead, at the end of the Ghoul's Ridge, you will see three blue lights at the summit. The first one to reach them will win the trial."

I looked over at the mountain summit. I could faintly make out blue, iridescent and flickering lights nestled in the rock that I hadn't noticed before.

This is too easy.

The ridge path to the lights was narrow, but it was clear and straight. I recalled the words Queen Trina had passed on to Ruby—that not all would be as it seemed. A sense of dread unfurled within me.

"There are no rules," the minister continued. "You know your task. When the horn sounds, the trial will begin."

The three champions positioned themselves at the start of the ridge, their bodies tense as they waited for the horn to sound. The crowd was completely silent, readying themselves to cheer on their hero when the trial began.

Just when I thought I was about to burst from the tension, the horn sounded, low and lingering. The champions sped off, just about keeping pace with one another as they ran along the ridge.

The crowed bellowed loudly, chanting Ash's name over and over again.

Ruby hurried over to me. "I don't get it."

"Me neither. Maybe there's a trap or something at the other end?"

We watched as all three made it to the halfway point of the ridge. Just then, a dark shadow ran over the grass in front of me, and I glanced up at the sky.

I only glimpsed the large, scaly talons of the vulture before they grabbed me by the collar and it lifted me clean off the ground.

"Hazel!" Ruby screamed, reaching out for my hand.

It was too late. Another vulture had grabbed her too, and we both hung in the air, our legs thrashing about wildly in panic. Nikolay's human was grabbed as well, and all three vultures soared upward.

The noise of the crowd echoed across the mountain range, mingling with my and Ruby's cries for help. The champions stopped still and stared, lips parted, as the vultures carried us swooping and gliding—circling around them.

Don't look down, whatever you do. Don't. Look. Down.

I looked down.

The drop had looked intimidating from the ground—now it made me almost pass out in a dead faint as its black, bottomless depths swam and blurred through my panicked vision.

I had never been so terrified in my life.

The vultures stopped their swooping and stayed positioned on either side of the ridge, in full view of the champions.

My eyes met Tejus's for a brief second before the talons of the vulture released me and I fell, hurtling through the air.

The Shade flashed across my mind. The thick forests, the sparkling lakes, the pristine beaches. The smile of my mother. Dad picking up Benedict and throwing him over his shoulder, both of them laughing. Our kidnapping from Murkbeech. Tejus standing at the window of the castle.

I'm not ready to go yet...

I closed my eyes, ready for oblivion.

Instead, I was yanked backward through the air, claws digging into my back, and then flying upward, away from the blackness below. The huge wings of the vulture flapped on either side of me till the pinnacle of the ridge and the waiting crowds started to grow closer.

I was dropped unceremoniously on the ground, where I collapsed. My heart pounding in my chest, I tried to catch my breath while I looked up at the blue sky above.

"What the *hell* are you doing!" Ash yelled at someone, and for a crazy moment I thought he was yelling at *me*.

I sat bolt upright, looking around for Ruby. I found her leaning upright against Ash, who was standing in front of the ministers, his face a puce red.

"You could have killed them!" he roared.

I staggered over to them and took Ruby's hand. She embraced me instantly, looking as dazed and confused as I felt. I looked over to the ridge, where Tejus and Nikolay were still running toward the blue lights.

"Oh, God. Where's Nikolay's human?" I breathed out.

Ruby looked at me in alarm, and simultaneously we rushed over to the edge of the mountain drop.

Sitting down, as if floating in mid-air, was Nikolay's human. He waved at us weakly, and I exhaled a sigh of relief. The ministers must have built an invisible barrier to catch us if we'd failed to be saved by our champions.

The realization that they weren't willing to let us die

comforted me a little, but not much.

"What do they think they're playing at?" Ruby hissed. "I'm sick to *death* of all this! I hate the ministers and the stupid trials! It's ridiculous!"

"Are you all right?" Ash had come over, having momentarily finished giving the ministers a piece of his mind.

"Not really," growled Ruby. "I can't believe they did this."

"And I've failed." Ash groaned. "I should have used mind manipulation on the vultures *while* I ran—not jumped on its back to get you."

"What are you talking about?" Ruby replied, shocked. "How could you have failed? You did the right thing— didn't you?"

Ash shook his head.

"Tejus will win. He saved Hazel without neglecting the task. *Succeed without losing one's sense of self,* remember?" he prompted.

"That's crap!" Ruby exploded. "You should be winning first place! The only one willing to sacrifice a stupid competition to save a life!"

I got what Ruby meant, but privately I agreed with Ash. As much as I hated to admit it, Tejus had done the right thing to win the trial. He had kept his eye on the prize. I didn't like the fact that I'd come second place, that the shock of seeing me drop through the air hadn't made him lose all sense of self-preservation and fly in gallantly to save me, but that was Tejus. He had told me he was selfish, that his needs would always come first. Why did I expect any different?

It must have been the adrenaline and the shock, but irrationally I wanted to cry—and I didn't want to be around Ruby and Ash for another second. Ash might have lost the trial, but he'd done what a resident of The Shade would do—put a life first.

He was more human than any of the other sentries I'd met.

I went to stand and watch the rest of the trial play out. Tejus and Nikolay were both flying back toward us on their vultures, each clutching bright blue egg-shaped stones in their hands.

Nikolay looked downcast. I shook my head in disgust. After this afternoon he'd plummeted in my estimation. He could say all the romantic sentiments and give me all the flowers on the earth, but it would never hide what he was. A monster.

"We have a winner!" the minister of ceremonies

announced as Tejus's vulture landed. "Tejus gains twenty points! Ashbik gains ten points for bringing back his human without the stone, Nikolay gains ten points for bringing the stone but no human. But alas, as Nikolay has the least points to date, our great and esteemed champion is now out of the running for the kingship trials. The last trial will be between Tejus and Ashbik alone!"

The crowd went berserk, chanting Ash's name once more, jubilant that their hero would be in the final tournament.

I just wanted to get out of here.

Turning away from the crowds, I went in search of Tejus's bull-horse. Soon I heard heavy footsteps and panting behind me.

"Hazel! Wait!" Nikolay called out to me.

I kept walking, utterly uninterested in anything he had to say.

"Wait—Hazel, I swear to you, I knew the barrier would be there." He had stopped in front of me, his hands on his knees as he caught his breath. "Think about it. My mother's a minister. I know how they think—I thought I would win if I got to the lights, and let my human fall...I wasn't thinking straight, you've got to believe me!" he pleaded.

"No, Nikolay, I don't have to believe you—and I don't. You're just like the rest of them," I sneered.

"Hazel, please—I promise you, I'm not the monster you think I am," he cried beseechingly, but I turned away.

"I've really had enough of sentries for today. Just leave me alone," I muttered, locating Tejus's bull-horse.

He didn't follow me. I didn't know whether I believed him or not, but right then I didn't care either way. Tejus's win felt like a hollow victory, and though it put him in the final trial with Ash, I just couldn't find it within myself to feel happy that freedom was in our reach—now, either way, we'd be out of here.

But I just felt empty.

JULIAN

I had escaped the servants' kitchen, where Ruby and Ash and all the kids were celebrating Ash's entry into the final trial, and stepped outside to get some air.

On hearing a blow-by-blow account of the insanely dangerous trial that Ruby and Hazel had just endured, and realizing that Tejus had won yet another tournament, my mind was made up.

Before the trial I'd overheard Tejus and Hazel discussing a mysterious stone when they thought they were alone in the courtyard. I'd hurried away before I could hear all of it – but I felt that I'd heard enough. Enough to tell Ruby at least – to level out the playing field.

Clearly Tejus was benefiting from some weird power the stone had given Hazel. It wasn't making it a fair fight, and if Tejus won the next trial, I still didn't trust him completely to set us all free when the Imperial trials would be up next. I also now knew enough about Nevertide to know that it needed a leader like Ash, not one like Tejus.

From every single angle, it felt like telling Ruby about the stone was the right thing to do.

When I got back inside, I saw Ruby sitting with Ash on the two large chairs by the fire while sugar-hyped kids sat around the counters and greedily ate everything in front of them. Jenney was running around looking harassed, mopping up spills and picking up rubbish. I hoped that if Ash became king Jenney would be able to live a life of leisure—weaving all day, or whatever it was sentries did when they weren't mind-sucking.

"Ruby, can I speak to you for a second?" I asked, approaching the chairs.

"What is it?"

"Let's go outside." I nodded to the doorway. I didn't want anyone else overhearing what I was about to tell her for Hazel's sake.

"Are you all right?" she inquired once we stood in the moonlight.

"Yeah, but I overheard something about the trials, about Tejus… and I think you should know."

I told her what I'd heard, and watched as Ruby's face fell on hearing about Hazel's part in it all.

"I can't believe she'd keep that from me," she whispered. "Are you sure you heard right?"

"Yeah. Pretty sure. You should speak to Hazel about it though—I dunno, maybe it was all a mistake," I replied lamely.

"Yeah, maybe," Ruby replied. I could tell she felt let down, and I kind of felt sick that I had been the messenger.

She went back inside, but I needed a few minutes by myself. For the first time since I'd arrived in Nevertide, the castle actually felt quite peaceful—out here at least. I leaned back against the stone walls and looked up at the huge blanket of stars that covered everything.

"Hey." Jenney stepped outside a moment later, wiping sweat off her brow. "I'm not disturbing you, am I?" she asked.

"No. I was just getting some fresh air," I replied.

"You do look kind of pale. Anything the matter?"

"No, not really. Looking forward to the final trial—and then getting out of here. Well, if Ash wins, that is," I replied.

"You don't think Tejus will lift the boundaries and let you go home?" she asked, evidently surprised.

"Err, no. He and his brothers kidnapped us in the first place, remember?"

"Yes," she replied slowly, "but I think he's a man of his word – and he did release you after the first trial. Perhaps you need to give him *some* credit. I'm not a fan of the Hellswan family, but Tejus is honorable. I know that much."

"I don't trust him," I replied bluntly.

"And maybe you shouldn't," Jenney replied. "I'm just telling you my experience." She shrugged.

Great. This really wasn't the best time for Jenney to suddenly become pro-Tejus. I was starting to feel guilty, and regretted sticking my oar in where it didn't belong.

"Still, I don't think you've got anything to worry about. Ash will stop at nothing to beat him."

The realization dawned on me. If Ruby told Ash he would almost definitely get Tejus disqualified from the trials. But that was a good thing, right?

Yeah, but you've betrayed Hazel—idiot.

I started pacing again. The decision I'd thought was so right didn't feel so black and white anymore.

But Hazel betrayed Ruby first, I told myself. *She kept the stone a secret!*

"Julian?" Jenney interrupted. "You've got to tell me what's going on. You never know, I might even be able to help." She smiled wryly, waiting for me to speak.

I couldn't tell her the whole truth, but maybe that didn't matter.

"I think I've stirred up stuff between friends. I heard parts of a conversation I shouldn't have—and passed it on. And I feel crappy about it." I sighed, running my hands though my hair in agitation.

"Only parts?" she asked.

"Yeah—but enough," I added defensively. "I got the gist of what they were saying."

"Did you check what the truth was before you passed on what you heard?" she asked.

"No," I replied. "I know what was said. I didn't need to!"

She grinned at me suddenly.

"Julian, you feel bad because you're not sure of the truth. When you're not sure of the truth, all you've done is pass on gossip. Do you want my advice? You need to go and tell whoever you overheard what you've done. Give them a heads-up at least—that would be the kind thing to do. If you're interested, that is."

She put a hand on my shoulder and gave me a quick squeeze before she went back inside.

I leaned back against the wall.

Dammit.

She was right. I needed to speak to Hazel.

Hazel

I spent the evening trying to avoid Tejus.

I could hear him moving about in the living room, but I stayed tucked away in the cubby hole. It reminded me of the night I'd been blackmailed by Jenus to kill him—hearing his movements and willing him to go to bed so that I could somehow pluck up the courage to stab him in the back.

This time it was me who felt betrayed.

It was silly—Tejus had done what the trial required, and he'd made sure that I was safe by mentally controlling the vulture to pick me up. But I couldn't escape the feeling that I'd been an afterthought, and for some reason it bothered me more than it should.

Ash sacrificed coming first to save Ruby.

It was a thought that kept going round and round in my head.

"Hazel? Are you awake?" Tejus peered in through the cubby hole.

"What do you want?"

"I need to go out for a while. I want you to stay here while I'm gone."

"Okay," I muttered.

"I won't be long." He started to shut the door.

"Leave it open," I commanded.

He reopened it and peered into my emerald-green gloom.

"What is wrong with you?" he asked, frowning. "You've been very quiet since we returned from the trial."

"I'm fine," I replied. "I'm just tired."

"I thought you'd be happy with the outcome." He looked at me quizzically. "You'll get to go home either way now."

"Yes, okay," I replied stonily. "As I said, I'm just tired."

He let out a sigh and rose up from his knees. A moment later I heard the door slam behind him.

I left the cubby hole, taking my blanket with me, and

curled up on the sofa. I wished, not for the first time, that I had my e-reader with me so I could escape into a reassuring and clichéd romance with a happy ending.

I was starting to doze off when I heard a knock at the door. I went to answer it, suddenly feeling nervous. I opened the door a crack, ready to jump back if I didn't like what I saw, but it was only Julian. I sighed with relief and swung open the door.

"What are you doing here so late?" I asked with concern. "Is Benedict okay?"

"He's okay," Julian hurried to reassure me. "It's just...I've got something to tell you that you're not going to be happy to hear."

"What's wrong?" I asked, instantly panicked.

"I overheard you and Tejus talking in the courtyard— about the stone." He looked shamefaced. "And I told Ruby. I'm so, so sorry, Hazel. I was worried that Ash wasn't going to win the trials...and we wouldn't get home."

Oh, crap.

"Does Ash know?" I asked.

"I don't know—I just told Ruby, but..." He left the rest of his sentence unfinished.

"You did tell her that I didn't use it in this trial though, right?"

"Um…no." He looked at the floor. "I didn't hear that bit."

"Right."

It was taking all my self-control not to throttle Julian right now.

"Look," I said, trying to maintain my calm, "I get why you did it, but I found the stone by accident. I didn't realize what it could do till later. And I never meant for it to give us a big advantage, it was more so I didn't get so tired. It was also what saved the other sentries from the disk. Had I not had the stone, Tejus wouldn't have stopped it in time."

He nodded. "I'm sorry. I didn't realize."

"It's okay." I sighed. "I'll sort it out with Ruby. Hopefully she won't tell Ash before I reach her."

After Julian left, I stood stone still in the middle of the living room, with a sick, queasy feeling in my stomach. If Ruby did tell Ash, then Tejus would be disqualified.

I should hide the stone.

It couldn't stay here—but where else would I put it? I didn't want to put it back in the sword. That would further implicate Tejus. And I didn't know where in the castle would be safe, too unfamiliar with anything outside of

Tejus's living quarters.

I could give it to someone—but who? It would have to be someone I trusted completely, but also who wasn't directly involved in the trials…

There was only one person I could think of, and that was my little brother.

I hurried into the cubby hole, hoping to get it to Benedict before Tejus returned. I would tell him the whereabouts of the stone *after* the last trial—I was afraid if I told him about Ruby knowing, he would take the stone back immediately and not let it out of his sight.

I placed the stone in my pocket and went off to find my brother.

He was in their living quarters, dozing on the sofa just like I had been moments before. I looked around for Ruby and Ash, but I couldn't see them anywhere.

Good.

"Benedict?' I shook him gently. "Wake up."

"Hazel?" He rubbed his eyes. "What are you doing here?"

"Can we go into your room?" I asked. "I want to talk to you about something."

"Okay," he murmured, looking at me with a small frown.

Once he'd shut the door, I sat down on the bed and beckoned for him to join me.

"I need to ask you for a favor—it's really important," I began. "I found a stone, a really powerful one, in Tejus's sword. I've been using it to help me in the trials, but if anyone finds out, or sees it in Tejus's possession, he's going to get disqualified from the trials. I was hoping you could look after it for me—keep it safe?"

"A-A stone?" Benedict asked, gulping.

"Yeah." I studied his expression, frowning. It was almost as if he was *afraid*. "Are you okay?"

"I don't know…" He hesitated.

"You're the only person I trust with this," I said, "and it's not harmful – maybe to sentries, I don't know – but not to us. I've been carrying it around for days."

He nodded, closing his eyes for a brief second before reluctantly holding out his hand.

"Benedict." I spoke softly, taken aback by his reaction. "You don't have to do this. I can put the stone somewhere else in the castle—it's okay."

"No, it's okay." He gave me a weak smile. "I've got a feeling it's my destiny."

I furrowed my brows at his odd response, then chuckled and ruffled his hair.

"Weirdo."

"I'll take good care of it. Won't let it out of my sight," he replied, much more confidently than before.

"Okay, thanks," I said, placing the stone in his hand. "And get some sleep. You look like crap."

He nodded and after I kissed his cheek goodnight I let myself out, feeling much lighter than I had when I arrived.

JULIAN

I punched my pillow in a huff, trying to get into a comfortable enough position to fall asleep. I wished I had my games console or a comic to help me zone out, but I had nothing to distract me from my guilty conscience or the new kid who snored like a rhino next door.

Lying on my back, staring at the ceiling, I started trying to estimate how many days were left until the barriers were lifted and we were able to get out of here. If the trial took place tomorrow, then I guessed there would be some kind of celebration or coronation-type thing, and then once Tejus or Ash were finally in charge, it would be time to go home. It could be as little as four days, three if we were lucky.

The thought was comforting—the end was in sight at last. Mostly I couldn't wait for my parents and the rest of GASP to get their hands on the sentry ministers and anyone else who thought kidnapping humans was a good idea. The look on Tejus's face when he realized that we were part of a global supernatural army was going to be priceless.

Finally, I began to grow drowsy, but a rustle coming from Benedict's bed made me look over to where my friend was sleeping.

Suddenly he sat bolt upright, shocking me so much my heart skipped a beat.

"Hell, Benedict—you scared the crap out of me!" I snapped at him.

He didn't reply.

"Benedict?" I questioned again, feeling uneasy.

He still didn't respond. His eyes were wide open, looking straight ahead, past me, to the wall. It was so freaky, him just sitting there, staring intently at the gray stone like he was watching something.

Still without speaking, he turned and slid out of his bed to stand in the middle of the room. I realized he was sleepwalking, but there was something about his face, half lit by the moonlight and half cast in shadow, that was making my blood run cold.

Without making a sound, he remained gazing ahead, expressionless.

I'd heard that you shouldn't ever wake a sleepwalker, but it took everything in my power not to do so—I *desperately* wanted him to go back to bed or wake up, or anything normal.

"Benedict...you're sleepwalking, wake up," I murmured softly, hoping that I might be able to reach his consciousness and feature as a voice of authority in whatever weird dream he was having.

Instead, he moved toward the door and twisted the handle slowly. When it swung open, he stood waiting in the doorway, facing the sleeping room of kids, without moving.

Goosebumps started to rise on the back of my neck.

Stop being so weird, Benedict.

I started to shuffle toward the end of the bed reluctantly. I didn't want to follow him, *at all*, but if he was going to go off somewhere in the castle then it was safer that I came with him—following at a distance.

With a sick feeling in my stomach, I watched him walk across the living room, miraculously avoiding stepping on the sleeping bodies, as if he was completely alert. Even I had trouble doing that in the dark, and ended up following him step by step so I didn't tread on anyone.

When he got to the main door, he pushed it open. I jumped to catch it before it shut behind him, and followed him out.

Our hapless guards were fast asleep, and the hallway that led to our quarters was deserted. Benedict kept walking in the direction of the belly of the castle, never hesitating, his footing sure and determined as if he knew *exactly* where he was going.

I followed a couple of paces behind, hanging back when he turned a corner or approached an arch. The more I watched him, the more adamant I became that he wasn't just mindlessly sleepwalking, but being drawn to some destination.

I wanted to know where.

I felt instinctively that there was something deeply wrong here. I just didn't understand what it was. I could only follow my friend.

As we continued our journey, I started to notice that every so often his left hand would reach down to feel about in his pocket... as if he was reassuring himself that something was there. I couldn't imagine what it might be though—these were the pants he'd slept in since we'd arrived, what could he possibly be keeping in them?

We turned down one hallway, and I started to recognize where we were. This was the corridor that had let to the closed-off passage, the one that Benedict had come running out of the time we went to find Hazel. I watched as he approached the small door and stood in front of it.

No. Don't go in there, Benedict.

It made me feel nauseous that in his sleep, Benedict would return to the place that had terrified him so completely when he'd been awake.

To my relief, he didn't open the door. He just stood there, like a statue, as if he were listening for something that only he could hear.

A moment later, he turned and continued back the way we'd come. I exhaled slowly—perhaps this would be the end of it? Maybe it was just that the corridor haunted his dreams so much that his body felt drawn to it, even in sleep.

Tomorrow morning, I was going to have a *long* chat with him—no way could this continue. It was the stuff of nightmares.

We turned another corner, and I could hear footsteps up ahead.

I backed up a bit so I was hidden by the wall, and hissed at Benedict to come back. I really didn't want him bumping into a sentry in this state, but he continued regardless, oblivious.

A plain-clothed figure entered the corridor, and as soon as it passed by a window, I exhaled with relief as the moonlight bounced off Ruby's blonde hair.

"Benedict?" she exclaimed. "What are you…"

I was about to step forward and explain the situation to her, but instead I froze, watching as Benedict reached into his pocket and brought out a strange-looking stone. Its color was electric in the gloom and it seemed to almost pulse with energy. He held it toward Ruby, his hand outstretched as if he were trying to hand it to her.

"Benedict!" she cried out.

A split second later she slumped to the floor, her head banging sharply on the stone floor.

I was so terrified it took a moment for my body to catch up with my impulse to rush forward. I half staggered into the hallway, but before I could take another step, something sharp and cold hit the back of my head with such force that I stumbled forward, too shocked to cry out. I felt hands roughly grab me from behind, dragging me backwards with a sharp jerk that almost took my arms right out of their sockets. I tried to struggle and twist around to see my attacker, but their grip was too tight and the more I fought against them, the more my vision started to swim and I started to get dizzy.

The last thing I saw before the world faded into a dark nothing was Benedict standing in the moonlit hallway. He slowly turned toward me, staring right at me. His expression was completely blank.

RUBY

I stood next to Ash in the arena where the first disk trial had been held. It wasn't good to be back.

The last time we were here, the sun had shone down brightly on the floor of the arena, bleaching out the sandy, yellow stone of the circular walls and the rings of bleachers that surrounded the dusty floor. Today though, it was gray—the sun had hidden behind a cloud, and off in the distance I could see thunderclouds that were almost black in appearance.

"Looks ominous, doesn't it?" Ash commented. "How are you feeling?"

"Been better… I just don't understand what happened,"

I replied, still trying to get my head around the events of last night and this morning.

I'd been woken early by two guards peering at me with concerned expressions on their faces. When I looked around, I'd found myself lying in the middle of a hallway in the castle, completely oblivious to how I'd gotten there. The last thing I could remember was going to find Hazel. It had been late, but I'd not been able to sleep after the conversation I'd had with Julian. I wanted to hear her side of the story and talk about what was going on—to either give her a piece of my mind, or find out that it was all a huge misunderstanding. All I knew was that I'd never reached Hazel...but there was something else I was missing—something that had happened before I could find her. I just couldn't for the life of me remember what it was.

"You probably fell," Ash replied, lifting his fingers to the very sore bump on my forehead, which I assumed was due to the stone floor.

"Wouldn't I remember that though?" I asked.

"Not necessarily if you were knocked out cold—it's lucky you didn't do any more damage to yourself, shortie. Wandering the castle at night? Never a good idea," he warned.

"Yeah, I know." I sighed.

The one thing I *wasn't* telling Ash about the incident was how weak I felt this morning. It worried me—I felt light-headed and drowsy, like I had absolutely no energy whatsoever left in me. As I returned to the living quarters and had breakfast, I'd kept hoping that I would get back to normal, but so far it hadn't happened.

And I was running out of time.

The trial would be starting in about an hour, and unless a vat of caffeine magically appeared before me, I was in trouble.

Unless...

I saw Hazel standing off on the sidelines with Tejus. She'd been avoiding me since we arrived and I hadn't been in the right frame of mind to speak to her either—but enough was enough. We needed to have this out, and I needed to get my energy back.

"Give me a minute," I said to Ash, and made my way over to where Hazel was standing.

Her face dropped as I approached, and she looked down at the ground, suddenly fixated on her sneakers.

"Can I speak to you for a moment please, Hazel?" I asked, eyeing Tejus coldly. He raised his eyebrows and then shrugged, backing off to go and stand by the arena walls, without taking his eyes off Hazel.

"Ruby," she whispered, "I know what you're going to say—and I'm *so* sorry—"

"What were you thinking?" I hissed back. "Was it that important to you that Tejus won?"

"No!" she cried, before adjusting her volume. "Sorry—no, it wasn't that important. I didn't understand how powerful it was till it was too late. I was only using it to replenish my energy. That's all. I'm really, really sorry—I should have spoken to you about it earlier."

"Damn right you should have," I snapped back at her. "Luckily for you, I hate it when we argue, and I've worked out how you can make it up to me."

"What? I'll do anything."

"I need the stone."

"What?" she asked, her mouth dropping open.

"I need the stone," I repeated slowly and firmly. "I went sleepwalking last night and hit my head on the floor. I feel like crap. Ash is relying on me—I need the stone."

"I don't have it," she whispered, glancing at Tejus.

"Does he?" I glared at her.

"No! He got mad when he realized I'd been using it. He made me keep it locked up in his cubby hole—but as soon as Julian told me that he'd told you about the stone, I moved it," she replied.

"Julian told you…?" I shook my head. "Forget it. Where did you put it?"

"I gave it to Benedict," she replied. "I thought that would be safest—so that Tejus wouldn't get disqualified."

I groaned. Benedict had remained behind at the castle. I'd seen him for breakfast this morning. *If only I'd known!* It was too late now. I wouldn't make it back in time for the start of the trial.

"I'm sorry," Hazel agonized.

"Well, I'm now also mad that you'd think I'd go running to Ash and we'd get Tejus disqualified. That's so low!" I exclaimed. "Do you really think I'd do something like that?"

Hazel shook her head. "I don't know what I was thinking. I guess I just panicked."

"Sentries!" The minister of ceremonies interrupted our argument in a loud, booming voice. "Welcome to the final installment of the kingship trials!"

The audience that had poured in since Hazel and I started talking cheered loudly and thumped their feet on the seats.

"The trial most of you have been waiting for—the one that truly tests the mettle of a king—the warrior trial!"

A RACE OF TRIALS

Again, the crowd erupted, sounding like a rabble of incensed beasts, and I winced at the blood-hungry undertones of their cries.

"Our two remaining champions—Prince Tejus, an advocate of industrious thinking, true wisdom and integrity, and Ashbik, an honest and talented champion, both willing to work together to achieve their goals—will now be pitted, one against one, as they battle for the crown of the kingdom!"

I surreptitiously rolled my eyes at the announcement. The ministers' obvious bias was starting to get to me. Hopefully after today, their loyalty would lie elsewhere, with Ash.

"Are you okay?" Ash turned to me.

"Yeah—I'm okay," I muttered.

"You just look exhausted. I'm worried that I've been draining you too much...and today? Tejus is the best sword fighter in all of Nevertide. I'll need you more than ever. I'm sorry, shortie. If it becomes too much— stop me. Okay?"

"Don't worry," I hastened to reassure him. "Take as much as you need. I'll be fine. You need to win this, Ash."

He nodded, and took my hand in his. I felt his thumb gently rub against my skin, making me feel warm all over.

We could do this. Together.

"The rules!" the minister shouted, trying to regain the attention of the crowd. "Champions will not be able to use mind powers on one another. The test is only of physical strength…this means no syphoning off either champion, no mind manipulation between the champions, and the wounds inflicted are not to be fatal. Of course, syphoning off your chosen humans is permitted. The first sentry on his back loses the trial, and you do not, on any account, leave the red-lined perimeter of the arena."

I looked down at the ground. Surrounding the center of the arena was a thick red circle of chalk, about the width of my palm. On the edges of the circle, red-robed watchers had positioned themselves about a meter apart.

"I've never seen so many of them," I whispered to Ash. "What are they doing?"

He watched them for a few moments, noticing their unmoving, expressionless forms.

"I guess they're there to make sure we don't step out of the line," he said. "Seems like a bit of overkill though."

I nodded. My thoughts exactly. Once again in these *stupid* trials, I doubted that all was what it seemed.

"Champions, enter the circle!" the minister announced grandly. "Wait for the horns!"

Ash squeezed my hand briefly and then stepped forward into the circle. Tejus entered the circle as well, and they slowly walked toward one another, meeting in the center of the arena.

Ash drew his broadsword from its scabbard, the pommel dark and worn with age, but the blade still powerful and deadly sharp. Tejus held the sword that he'd won from his father at the labyrinth, the sword of Hellswan. It glinted dangerously, ornate and bejeweled, but its blade uncompromised, and no doubt made from the best steel that money could buy.

The horns sounded, low and booming across the hollow of the arena. My gut clenched, and I sent out a prayer that Ash made it out of this alive.

Ash was the quickest to respond. He swiped his sword at Tejus, who blocked it forcefully—a clash echoed. As Tejus blocked the onslaught, he pushed forward, making Ash take a step back to regain his footing. Tejus raised his sword up high, then brought it down, aiming for Ash's arm. The blades locked together once again, and Ash pushed off.

A rhythm started to emerge. Both men were well matched. Tejus was clearly the warrior with better precision and style, but Ash's build and strength seemed to make up for the rest.

They grunted and heaved, each blow clashing, steel on steel, creating a grating sound that pierced my eardrums and made me wince. As they moved in a guarded, circular motion, my heart felt like it was in my throat. I waited for the familiar feel of Ash reaching out for me with his mind, but it didn't come.

A few moments later, I began to realize that both Tejus and Ash were starting to grow tired. The blows came with less speed, and then with less force. They were both sweating heavily, their grunts of effort grew louder. With the crowd waiting in absolute silence, and not so much as a breeze evident, their heavy panting soon became audible and it was almost as if I could *feel* the effort it took Ash to raise his arm to block or parry each blow.

I was confused as to why the battle was taking this much out of them, and why their energy seemed to have disappeared almost in an instant.

They're being drained.

I looked around at the red robes who surrounded the circle. Their gazes were fixed intently on the champions, unwavering. No wonder they were growing tired! The red robes were siphoning off their energy—and there wasn't a thing either of them could do about it.

Ash, siphon off me!

I tried to create a connection with him myself, reaching out for his mind so that he could take what little I had to give.

It was no use—nothing was happening.

Whenever I felt the connection of our energy start to intertwine, mine would fade out, and Ash would be left unable to grasp onto anything. But he continued to fight, heaving his entire body weight into every blow against Tejus.

Looking over at Hazel, I could see that Tejus was siphoning heavily off her, but she was starting to fade. She swayed slightly as she stood at the periphery of the circle, her eyes fixed determinedly on her champion.

Why can't I do this?

I re-focused, trying with all the energy I had to reach out to Ash, to give him *something*, anything I had left.

It wasn't enough.

I could see Ash's focus slipping away. When Tejus brought down his sword now, Ash's blocks were slower, the blade closer to his body. He was bleeding heavily from his arm, and I could see another gash in his leg.

Tejus looked monstrous, his dark features pronounced as his face screwed up in fury and the same look of determination that Hazel wore. He had a deep cut across his cheekbone, covering one side of his face in a dark crimson.

Please, hold on, Ash, keep going!

"Come on, Ash!" I cried out loudly. If I couldn't give him my mental energy, then I was going to give him his own cheerleading section. The crowd started to murmur, and then my cries were joined by theirs—

"Come on, Ashbik! Win for us!" and, "Keep going—end the Hellswan!"

Most of the crowd were up on their feet now—tense, anxious—desperately wanting their chosen champion, the champion of the people, to pull through.

He fought harder. It was killing him. His pale face was even whiter than usual, his eyes a bloodshot red as the siphoning took effect.

Ash rallied for one last blow. With both hands he clutched at his sword, and with a loud, brutal cry he brought the blade down with a swoosh.

Tejus blocked it, but Ash held fast, both blades inching steadily toward Tejus's neck. A brief look of triumph passed through Tejus's features as he suddenly, violently threw the blades back, knocking Ash to the ground.

It was done.

Tejus held the tip of his sword at Ash's neck.

"A good fight," Tejus breathed heavily, "you put up a good fight."

No!

The crowd fell silent, and it was only the ministers who applauded Tejus's win with an enthusiastic, though restrained, round of hand-clapping.

Tejus held out his hand to Ash, who took it and let his opponent pull him to his feet. Ash's face was downcast, and when he stood his shoulders were slumped in defeat. I couldn't bear to watch.

Out of the corner of my eye I saw the minister of ceremonies take the podium. He stood right by the royal box, where Queen Trina looked murderous.

I couldn't hang around to hear the sycophantic praise from the minister.

Turning toward the entrance, I set off at a run, moving as fast as my stupid, de-energized body would carry me.

"Ruby!" Ash called after me, but I was gone.

I ran into the forest, needing to be alone and as far away from the sounds of the arena and the voices of the smug, self-satisfied ministers within it.

Finding a fallen log, I slumped down on it, placing my head in my hands. I sat for a moment, listening to the silence of the forest and my gasping breath.

It wasn't long before I heard a thrashing coming from the undergrowth toward me, footsteps slow and labored. I looked up in time to see Ash move a branch out of his way and step into the clearing where I was sitting.

"What are you doing?" he panted.

"Ugh! I'm so sorry. I completely failed you."

He continued walking, even slower but just as determined. His shirt was soaked in blood and sweat, and his body heaved painfully with every step he took, blood slowly seeping from his cuts.

"It's my damn fault you lost. I couldn't—"

"Ruby. Shut. Up," he interrupted, taking a final step toward me.

He yanked me roughly upward from the log and held me fiercely in his arms, his eyes looking straight into mine, boring into me.

I opened my mouth to speak again, but as I did so, his lips met mine with a low groan—forcing me silent.

Oh.

He kissed me, bruising my lips with his force, until his arms wrapped around my frame. I felt dizzy, like the ground was falling away beneath my feet—but Ash held me so tightly it didn't matter. I could have been falling through air and still have felt like I was anchored safely. My arms tentatively reached upward, across his broad back to feel the trembling skin beneath the fabric of his shirt.

"Ouch," he breathed out, breaking his lips from mine and running them gently across the skin of my cheek.

"I'm sorry," I whispered back.

"You have nothing to apologize for. I would never have gotten this far without you."

His lips found mine again, this time gentler and sweeter, showing me that it was okay, that all that mattered was us—in this moment, with the crowds, the ministers and the trials fading into the distance.

I let it all go, and drowned in the increasing crush of his kisses, while answering them with my own.

HAZEL

I had taken over Tejus's bedroom for the afternoon, at his request, while two servants helped me prepare for the coronation ceremony. One was a glum-faced old woman who hadn't looked me in the eye all day, but the other was a younger, smiling creature who seemed to be bubbling over with excitement.

I was sitting at a vanity mirror, an item brought in for the occasion, while my hair was combed and pulled into an appropriate style befitting a friend of "his royal highness", King Tejus of Hellswan.

After Tejus had won the trials, and the ministers had finished crowding round him and congratulating him while the 'commoner' crowd of sentries had trickled off, downhearted and grumbling, Tejus and I had returned to the castle to have someone tend to the wounds Ash had inflicted. Too tired to do much else, I had gone to bed.

When I woke, my surroundings had changed—I was no longer in the small cubby hole that I'd fallen asleep in, but instead I found myself in one of the guest bedrooms in Tejus's quarters. I wondered who had put me in here, but I'd not seen Tejus all morning to ask. Only the servants had appeared, and I hadn't seen anyone else.

I should have taken a trip down to see Ruby. She had run off after the trial before I could stop her, disappointed with their loss. But before I could do so, the servants had entered the room and practically forced me into a hot bath.

"Are you excited?" the servant girl asked quietly, out of the elder woman's hearing.

"I'm excited to be going home," I said. "They'll lift the barriers soon and I'll be able to return to my dimension."

She frowned. "Oh. You're not going to stay?"

"This isn't my home. I want to see my parents. It was the deal I made with Tejus in return for helping him."

"But don't you *want* to stay with the king?" she replied, apparently shocked.

I thought she might have the wrong idea about our

relationship, and I hesitated before replying.

"My friends and I… we just want to go home."

She nodded, the excitement in her eyes dulling as she digested my news. After a few moments she brightened again. "Well, I loved watching the two of you in the trials. You made such a good team. Don't you think he's so *handsome?*" She giggled, and covered her mouth.

Handsome?

Um… Yes, he was. I found him more attractive than I was ready to admit. But he was arrogant, selfish and egotistical too. I felt like I might always have something of a bond with Tejus—we'd been through too much together for me not to feel that way—but I also knew that my feelings toward him were complicated; his mood swings and general surly, calculating demeanor were not things I would miss. Neither would I miss the roller-coaster rides of emotion he brought up in me—furious the one minute, and then feeling almost affection the next as he battled his demons at every turn of the trial—a broken family, spiteful ex-girlfriend, and most of all himself.

"He is," I replied to the servant girl.

It had been the right answer. She continued to work on my hair, her face pink with excitement as she twisted and pinned it up into an elaborate hairdo.

Next came the dress. It was brought up by two other servants, and there was lots of fussing and inspecting of the needlework. I felt hugely uncomfortable while all this was going on—I was starting to feel like a bride on the day of her wedding, and was totally overwhelmed by all the attention. I started to wonder what would be expected of me at this coronation…I was hoping to be able to blend into the background, but as soon as I caught sight of the dress I realized that would be highly unlikely.

The bodice was almost sheer gold silk, with artfully placed lace flowers to protect my modesty. It flowed down to a long gown of the same silk, which rippled across the floor—covered in the same lace flowers, thousands of them, woven into the dress. I had also been given a pale white cape, its fabric similar to the smoothest suede, with soft, gray lining.

I crossed my arms.

"What's wrong?" asked the youngest servant girl.

"Well, it's beautiful, but… it's just too much."

"But King Tejus ordered this for you. It's made to your measurements exactly. You *have* to wear it," she pleaded.

"I don't mean to be ungrateful…but isn't there something a bit plainer I could wear?" I asked.

"No." The girl looked downcast again. "We'll get into

trouble if this gown isn't worn. I don't think the king would be happy with us."

I rolled my eyes. She'd played her trump card. I couldn't let a bunch of sentries who'd tried to help me get in trouble—especially with Tejus new to his role. If he wanted to change the reputation of the Hellswans, stuff like this would matter.

"Okay," I agreed reluctantly, making a mental note to have a word with Tejus about this later. "Let's try to get it on…" I looked doubtfully at the gown—it looked so small, and had no obvious openings. Would they have to *sew* me into the thing?

Miraculously, only a few minutes later I was dressed. They brought me a full-length mirror, and I stopped dead when I saw myself. Well, it hardly seemed to be me. I looked like some fairy princess, totally unrecognizable— and totally uncomfortable with the transformation. There was something about the intricate detail and the immaculate coloring and finish of the gown that made me want to run off and find my Chucks and my most comfortable sweats.

"Here, try the cape." The girl rushed forward and threw the article over my shoulders. This was an item I could get behind. It was so soft and luxurious, and kept the near-constant chill of the castle at bay.

"I like this... Thank you."

"You look beautiful," she replied. "Like sentry royalty!"

No, thanks.

I covered up my disdain with a smile, and realized that my jaw was going to be aching for the rest of the day with faux-smiles and nodding along to praise directed at Tejus.

A moment later, the servants scuttled from the room as if they'd all simultaneously heard some unspoken command, and Tejus walked in.

He stopped in the doorway, his gaze taking in my hair and the gown and then swiftly settling on the view from his bedroom window.

Charming.

"You look... different," he managed eventually.

"So do you." He was dressed in the robes I had seen his father wear—a dark crimson red, embroidered with golden thread. Rings adorned his fingers, and he looked the part—the cold, distant king of Hellswan.

"I hope the ceremony will be brief," he replied, changing the subject, "I want you to sit by my side at the throne. It's a non-negotiable request," he added, before I could protest, "the last one I will make of you before you're free."

I stared at him stonily, angry that another demand was being made of me against my will.

"Hazel… I need you there," he said.

"Can you not ask someone more suitable to join you? Like Queen Trina, for instance?" I asked before I could stop myself.

He frowned, confused.

"Why would I ask her?"

"Oh, I don't know—wasn't my attempted *kidnapper* your past girlfriend or whatever?" I bit out.

I didn't know why I said it. I supposed I was just sick of so many unsaid things between us—the stone, the queen, the integrity trial. Now that the pressure of the trials were over, I wanted answers.

"So you overheard that," he replied after a pause.

"I was looking for you. Why didn't you tell me? Don't you think I should have known that I needed to be wary of her?"

"She wasn't a threat. I would never have let her harm you." He stopped talking for a moment and looked at me with raised brows. "Is this what you've been so angry about all this time? That you thought I wasn't protecting you?"

"No."

Yes.

"I was annoyed you'd been keeping secrets from me, especially after you gave me such a hard time over the stone. And I wasn't impressed with the integrity trials—I could have *died* and your only concern was winning."

He looked taken aback by my unexpected revelations... and to be honest, so was I.

"You weren't going to die. You know that. I knew that. The ministers aren't quite the monsters you think they are, Hazel. The trial was about balancing the interests of the kingdom with personal ones—I did what was right." He stared at me, his expression adamant.

I didn't know what to say. His arguments seemed perfectly reasonable—but it still didn't help the way I felt.

A silence fell between us, during which I avoided Tejus' gaze. Then he broke it. "We need to leave. Are you ready?"

I nodded.

He walked over to me slowly, and held his arm out. I wondered what he was doing for a split second before I understood that he meant for me to take it and walk down with him.

"It's appropriate," he muttered.

I laid my hand on his upper arm, my body brushing against his. Despite everything, his nearness seemed to be helping my nerves. If I was going to have to face a room full of ministers and sentries, Tejus would still be my first choice of companion.

* * *

The coronation was uneventful.

I'd been guided—or manhandled, depending on your perspective—to the throne next to Tejus's. It was hard and uncomfortable, with a tall gilded back which matched the opulence of the rest of the building. The ceremony had taken place in what reminded me of a church—joined to the castle by a long hallway I'd never seen before. Only the ministers were present, and none of the townspeople or the rest of my friends.

"Don't leave my side," Tejus murmured before the ceremony began. I couldn't help but notice how tight-lipped and pale he looked. I suspected the truth of it was that he was nervous. Instead of reassuring him again that I had no intention of "leaving his side", I placed my hand over his for a moment. He didn't say anything, or even look in my direction, but I noticed his muscles relaxed.

The ceremony took a little over an hour, and at the end, Tejus was presented with the crown of Hellswan. It looked like it weighed a lot.

Uneasy is the head that wears the crown. I recalled a quote from Shakespeare. It seemed apt in this moment. Tejus might have appeared outwardly calm to the onlookers, but I doubted he felt that way on the inside.

Tejus and I were led, as part of a mini-procession, back into the main part of the castle to where the banquet and celebrations would be held.

We were in the same room where the championship dinner had taken place, but the decorations this time were far more extravagant. Everywhere I looked I could see dark crimson and gold—from the chair throws to the table runners and the ornate display pieces. The doors were once again opened into the gardens, and torches blazed from every available surface, and great big bonfires had been lit at various points across the lawn. While I admired the effort, it did make me feel like I was standing in the middle of some hellish inferno.

"Bit much, don't you agree?" A voice sounded from behind me.

Nikolay was standing on the patio, his handsome face in a hopeful half-smile.

"I don't want to have anything to do with you," I retorted.

"Hazel, give me a chance. I swear to you, I knew my human wasn't in danger. My mother has been helping me throughout the trials. Me winning meant everything to her. Forgive me, Hazel. I'm not your enemy, and I imagine in Nevertide you have enough of those."

I couldn't bring myself to get into an argument. I let out an exasperated sigh, and looked around for Ruby or Benedict to save me, but I hadn't seen them since I'd arrived.

"How about a dance?" Nikolay asked.

You're pushing your luck.

I was about to say no when Tejus stepped out of the shadows and came to stand next to me—his tall frame towering menacingly over both Nikolay and me, his face half lit by the fires that surrounded us.

"Nikolay, I was made king ten minutes ago," Tejus said, his voice dangerously low, "and you have the rare fortune to be the subject of my very first decree. Stay away from this young woman, or you'll end up in the Hellswan dungeons, many, many miles from a mirror."

Nikolay looked at me, and then at Tejus. He bowed swiftly, mortified, and turned on his heel, walking back indoors.

I didn't miss a small smirk cross Tejus's lips.

"That was a bit unnecessary," I muttered to him once Nikolay was out of earshot, not quite willing to let on that

I was relieved by the interruption.

"No, it wasn't," he replied crisply. "You are worth a thousand of him. He's not fit to breathe the same air as you, Hazel. Choose your companions better."

As Tejus took my arm and led me out of the hall and onto a torchlit balcony—away from the bustle of the crowd—I marveled at how he could turn such a flattering and unexpected compliment into an insult. I didn't know what to say, other than to make a snarky remark about my 'companions' being my own choice, but I decided against it. I didn't want to argue with Tejus anymore this evening. We should be celebrating and congratulating one another on getting this far, not taking cheap snipes and arguing.

"How does it feel?" I asked, diverting the conversation as I rested my hands on the balcony's ornately carved stone railing.

"To be king?" he questioned grimly. His eyes trailed over the dark horizon. "I'm not sure. I suppose... it feels like I've followed in the steps of my father... That I've done the right thing by my family name."

I looked up at him, slightly taken aback by the honesty of his answer—and his resigned tone. The eyes that met mine were determined and assured, but for the first time I got the impression that at least part of that was a veneer.

There was something about Tejus this evening, which I'd first glimpsed at the coronation too, that felt lost and uncertain.

"And what about what *you* want?" I asked quietly.

"That is irrelevant. Particularly now." He smiled ruefully. "I have lived a privileged life in many respects, but the luxury of choice has always evaded me."

His words reminded me of the conversation I'd overheard between him and Queen Trina—how she'd accused him of abandoning her when he had put his family, and his father, first.

"I'm not sure I believe you…" I hesitated, knowing that I might well be overstepping the boundaries of our complicated friendship. "I think we always have a choice," I dared say, recalling my grandma Sofia's famous words— words that had become a family motto. "Every single one of us. It's just that there are consequences to every choice we make, and some are easier to live with than others." I thought of the choice I had deliberated over, the killing of Tejus to save my brother—one that had appeared so black and white at first, so obvious, but when it had come down to it, I had faltered.

He was looking at me questioningly, but didn't seem irritated, so I continued.

"I think that sometimes it's easier to pretend that we don't have a choice, so we don't have to stand up for what we really want—and live the lives we want to live. We're afraid."

He took a step closer to me, his eyes almost luminous in the firelight. He had never looked less human to me— large and looming, his figure dwarfing mine and the long scar that faintly marked his cheekbone from the fight with Ash making him appear more deadly than ever.

My heart skipped a beat as he raised his hand. I stood unmoving before him, like prey and predator before the final strike. But instead of acting in anger, he brought his hand down slowly, tenderly grazing his thumb along the frame of my face.

"And what would I choose?" he asked, his expression serious.

I swallowed, momentarily forgetting how to breathe as my skin tingled where his skin had touched mine.

"What would I have instead of my crown?" he asked again.

"I don't know," I whispered.

He drew in closer, and I felt like I was becoming consumed by his presence, hyper-aware of the intensity that radiated off him, the broad torso that stood unmoving in front of me, trying to ignore the small voice in the back of my head that warned me away from him—just as every single nerve in my body urged me closer. Usually when we were this…*intimate*, we were mind-melding or he was siphoning off me. This was different—our closeness was taking on a new dimension, and a completely new direction—one I hadn't really been willing to admit to myself that I wanted.

Until now.

"Don't you?" he breathed. His right hand moved slowly up and touched my face as he looked searchingly into my eyes.

I couldn't answer him, and he smiled softly, almost sadly at my silence.

"I wonder sometimes, if I had known you long before now, if I would find this place so black." As he spoke, the bonfire near us flared then dimmed, casting Tejus in almost complete darkness. The next moment, I felt the soft, cool skin of his lips brush against my own, so fleetingly I thought I'd imagined it.

I moved closer to him, desperately wanting his touch to return. Instead, he groaned softly against the nape of my neck, the chill of his breath sending shivers running up and down my spine.

"Please," I whispered, hardly knowing what I was asking for. I felt his body tense in response, his fingers digging into my arms. His forehead came to rest on mine, his eyes closed, both of us breathing shallowly.

"Hazel—I…"

He didn't finish his sentence. Instead, a low growl tore from his throat, and his lips pressed against my half-open mouth. Even as he succumbed to the thing he wanted in that moment, me, I knew that he felt he had lost a battle – that in this instance Tejus was giving in, surrendering something to me that he'd tried his hardest to hold at bay.

The sweet and fleeting brush of his skin flittering on mine moments earlier was replaced by something urgent and more wanting. As he wound his hands into my hair clutching me to him, his body created an unbreakable barrier around mine. I felt the warm tip of his tongue delve between my lips, and I inhaled the taste of his mouth – my senses becoming drugged as our kiss deepened and became the pivotal point of my existence – the cold night air, the fires and the quiet murmurings of the distant sentries, they all meant nothing as I clung to Tejus, already dreading the moment he would release me.

His hands roamed firmly over my body, running up and down my back – causing my entire being to tremble, each touch burning the same way my cheek had. I shivered uncontrollably, and he tightened his grip further, bringing me closer to his muscular frame and the thundering of his heart. His body was hard and unyielding, his torso like stone against my softer skin, but even so it brought me comfort, and the countless times I had been pressed against him for protection – the flights on vultures, in the aftermath of the disk trial, being released in the forest – flashed through my mind. As strange and euphoric as I felt with my blood soaring through my body, and all the breath pushed out of me and relinquished to him, I felt completely safe, knowing that within Tejus's grasp, nothing could harm me.

Tejus broke the kiss, holding me away from him.

Except that.

"I can't -" His breath was ragged and labored. I looked up at him in confusion, and in that moment I saw a flash of fear cross his face. Fear was something I'd never seen Tejus exhibit before – not even in the caves.

"No, please, speak to me," I croaked, my voice barely above a whisper.

"This is wrong," he breathed. "I'm sorry -"

"Hazel!" Ruby cried out across the balcony.

I jumped back from Tejus, still catching my breath. I

suddenly felt violently cold, as if I'd just stepped outside in the middle of winter.

What did he mean?

I glanced back at Tejus, but he didn't meet my eye. He stared off, past Ruby, and I could see the effort it was taking him to reign back whatever it was he wanted to do, or say in that moment.

"Thank God I found you. I've been looking everywhere!" Ruby barely looked in Tejus's direction, oblivious to what she'd just interrupted.

She was rushing toward us, and behind her, Jenney and Benedict appeared too, looking as anxious as Ruby, their breath coming in short pants as they approached.

"We can't find Julian! He's vanished!" Ruby panted.

"He's been missing since this morning," Jenney said, "no one's seen him."

"And last night?" I asked, panic taking a hold of me.

Benedict looked at Jenney, who shook her head.

"We went to bed at the same time," Benedict replied hoarsely, "but when I woke he wasn't there." He blanched, and I went over to clutch my brother's shoulder, hoping to comfort him.

"He's got to be *somewhere*!" I said.

"I don't even know where to start." Ruby's tone was

frustrated and angry. "Ash is searching the servant quarters as we speak, but I'm not holding out much hope—I'm worried Julian's left us. That he doesn't *want* to be found," she added quietly.

"What?" I exclaimed. "He wouldn't abandon us!"

I thought about the awkward position I'd put Julian in because of the stone, and how none of us had taken his declarations about finding our own way out of Nevertide seriously. Had we alienated our friend that much?

I looked to Tejus. "Please, will you help us find him?" I breathed, flushing as our eyes met.

Tejus's face had assumed a stony mask, his mind and emotions once again under full control. He merely pursed his lips, swiftly avoiding my direct gaze. It was as if it was a different person standing before me now than just a few moments ago.

"I must discuss the matter with the ministers," he replied after a short pause, as he shifted his focus to the banquet hall.

It was the response of a king, not a friend.

"What do you mean?" I asked, frowning.

"You seem to forget that I am a ruler now," he replied, his voice distant. "King Tejus of Hellswan, and now contender to Nevertide's emperorship. I cannot expend our guards flippantly—especially not the number you'd require to find a human so thoroughly lost that his closest companions couldn't locate him... Every action I now take must be in the kingdom's best interest, not just your own."

I stared at him, my mouth drying out.

What's happening to him?

Is this *the choice he's making?*

"Of course," Ruby retorted angrily, "we'd never expect the 'king of Hellswan' to help us out of the goodness of his heart," she spat. "You only ever promised to let us free in the first place because it was in your interest."

Tejus didn't rise to Ruby's jab. He merely ignored her.

I could hardly bear to look at him.

I'd tried to begin explaining to Tejus that he had choice, that he did not *have* to become a hollow, carbon copy of his father and follow in his bleak footsteps. But he hadn't given me enough of a chance. Enough *time*. A switch had flicked in him too soon, and now I feared there might be no going back.

His kiss... had that been some sort of good bye? Had he already made up his mind as to his destiny, and his caress was like a final, hopeless reach for what I sensed he wanted, deep down—to feel, to connect... *To love?*

Now it felt like a barricade had closed down around him, as impenetrable as the barriers that surrounded this joyless, shadowed empire. That all that existed in his world was himself and his newly acquired power. That he was no longer a friend or…whatever we were, but a man responsible for the rule of his people, and—more importantly in Nevertide—navigating the fraught political landscape of ministers and combative queens.

"Come on, Hazel." Ruby's voice broke through my wilderness of thoughts. "Whatever *he* ends up doing, all we can do is keep searching for Julian ourselves in the meantime." She tugged at me, dragging me away with Jenney and Benedict, and I followed, my legs feeling like dead weight.

Before we re-entered the banquet hall, I looked back fleetingly. Tejus was still standing at the edge of the balcony, the remaining firelight dancing across his broad back, the breeze carrying his dark hair. He cut a lonely figure, despite the distinct aura of wealth and power surrounding him.

In that moment, it felt like Julian wasn't the only friend I'd lost tonight.

TEJUS

You fool.

I watched as Hazel was dragged away by her friend, and like a coward I was relieved that I wouldn't have to explain myself further – that I wouldn't have her standing in front of me, relentlessly tempting my baser urges.

How much would you take from her, Tejus?

Was it not enough that I'd taken her from her home, selfishly for my own purposes – disregarding her needs, desires and wants – and worse, that I'd put her within reach of my morally repugnant family and Queen Trina Seraq?

And now...Now was I willing for her to pay the

ultimate price, because I was too selfish to refuse her for a moment longer?

Had I known, long ago, when my father first commanded us to take our pick of the minds from the human world to help in the upcoming trials, that I would return with its brightest and most brilliant creature, would I have disobeyed him then?

No. I doubted that I would have.

I would have taken her anyway, and proceeded to do what I was doing now – crushing the spirit of a girl so bright, she put my darkness to shame.

Had she been any different, less honorable, less brave and loving toward her family, I would have claimed her as my own in a heartbeat – which had been my intention from the start, as soon as I realized how powerful her mind was.

But I had developed…*feelings* for her.

At first they had seemed inconsequential – we were working together, closely, and a certain bond could emerge through repeated mind-melding, I was no stranger to that. But it had intensified; I had started to concern myself with her opinion of me – far more than I should. When she had trembled as we flew on my vulture, I had wanted to quell her fears. When I realized that she had been bound and blindfolded in the forest, I had wanted to destroy the land till I found her – annihilating everything that had stood in my way. She had accused me of not caring of her safety during the trials at Ghoul's Ridge – how wrong she was. I had hesitated; almost lost precious moments when I'd seen her falling through the air, and it had taken all of my will to keep running and not turn back, even though I knew she would be safe. It was one of the hardest things I'd ever done. I was drawn to her, always. Her entire being seemed to taunt me. Every so often I would glance her way, and become transfixed by her hair, her eyes, the way her nose wrinkled when she was concentrating, or how she would chew her lip when she was nervous. Soon I had begun to realize that she saw me in a way that no other had ever done. It became harder to keep up my mask of indifference, and every time I hurt her, I felt like the most despicable being in this world.

Had my feelings remained just warm, I would have given her all that I could provide: the greatest riches of Hellswan – and eventually the whole of Nevertide – wealth beyond her wildest imagining, a kingdom laid at her feet to command... all that any female could possibly want. How beautiful she'd looked tonight, dressed as she ought to be, in the softest silks and finery I could provide. But to

Hazel, all of those promises would be hollow – more so once she understood the true terms of any kind of contract between us. I didn't know how I'd even begin to tell her. What would someone so young, so *human*, understand about our archaic rules? It was law here that a sentry of royalty could only marry one of his or her own kind. To become a match for me, Hazel would have to surrender herself completely.

She'd have to become a sentry.

And what would I give her in repayment for a metamorphosis she would find so reprehensible? I had nothing of real value to offer – my soul a dead thing, my selfishness and my self-will would strangle the life out of her, drag her down into my own bleak depths.

"You look dejected for a man just crowned."

I spun around, angry at the intrusion, before my eyes lighted on Commander Varga's familiar silhouette. He was dressed in the full uniform of the Royal Guard, a sight rare for the commander, who preferred to dress beneath his station, always claiming that the battlefield held no regard for rank – a dead man was a dead man.

"Not at all," I replied, dismissing my somber thoughts. "What of the boundaries?"

The commander shook his head. "They have already

been lifted around Hellswan. But there is a problem. The ministers of the other kingdoms have been trying to remove the larger barrier around Nevertide, and thus far have been unable to lift it."

"Was it our ministers who put it in place?" I asked swiftly.

"Acting on your father's orders, yes," he replied grimly.

"Perhaps they are needed to remove it, in that case."

This was far from ideal. For my own personal reasons, which I didn't want to divulge to Varga, I wanted the barriers removed tonight. I couldn't have Hazel around Hellswan any longer. It was time to set her free, before I willingly lost myself and destroyed her in the process. I idly wondered if she and the other humans could be moved to another kingdom. But I quickly dismissed it. It was far too risky. She needed to get out of Nevertide.

"Are our ministers making their way to the Nevertide border to investigate?" I asked.

"Yes, along with a few guards"

I nodded. "Good. Let me know the moment the situation is resolved."

"Of course. In the meantime, new king, enjoy tonight. Were you just talking to your human – what was her name, Hazel?" Varga continued, his tone implying that he was just making conversation, but I bristled at the idea that anyone might have witnessed our exchange.

"Hazel," I confirmed. "I was."

"She's quite impressive," he replied mildly. "I saw her in the trials. She must have been a great help."

I nodded curtly, wondering why the normally perceptive Varga wasn't abandoning his line of enquiry completely.

He smiled. "I thought that perhaps, you and her might..."

"Don't think on it." I glowered at him, daring him to further the conversation.

"Tejus, you need a wife," he pressed. "The ministers would be in uproar, of course, but I thought that might please you, perversely ... as long as she was willing to pay the price, of course."

"Not her," I snapped back.

Varga looked at me questioningly, but then remained silent. I turned to look out over the balcony, watching the flames of the bonfires roar below.

"Then perhaps you'll take back Queen Trina..." Varga continued, a touch of hesitation in his voice.

"Perhaps. Why this incessant line of questioning, Commander?" I asked, belatedly realizing that he wouldn't be so insistent with the conversation if there wasn't a true need behind it.

Varga sighed. "It's the ministers, and the imperial trials. You know how biased they can be – you saw it for yourself during the kingship trials. If you took a wife, the ministers would favor you more greatly. Both King Thraxus and Memenion are your age, and are already wed. They will be your stiffest competition for the position of Emperor."

I snorted with derision.

"Those men are inadequate. Queen Trina even more so – but she is more devious, of course," I replied with a smirk.

"Will you let your arrogance rule you, Tejus?" Varga retorted.

I smiled at him slowly.

"Be careful how you address me, old friend," I warned.

"Forgive me, Tejus," Varga sighed. "I only want to see you at your father's thrones – both as king and Emperor."

I nodded, we both knew he was forgiven. There were few in Nevertide that I could trust – fewer still that I could bear to exchange more than a few words with, but Commander Varga was the exception. He had grown up in this castle, his father a great friend of my own. At first we had been united by our hatred of Jenus, and later our friendship, if I could call it that, had grown out of a mutual respect. We were an unlikely pair, even I could see that. Varga was generous and open-minded, whereas I knew my shortcomings enabled me to be anything but.

"I will leave you in peace, but think on what I've said. You were born for this Tejus – no matter what your father may have thought."

He turned and left the balcony, and I remained alone.

What was it that Hazel had said, that I was 'afraid' to make choices? I laughed into the darkness. There wasn't one in the entirety of Nevertide who would have dared insult me so thoroughly to my face.

But perhaps she had been right. I had spent years training and preparing myself for the trials in every way imaginable, ignoring the fact that my father preferred Jenus – knowing full well that my odds of besting him with my father's aid would have been slim. Not once had I questioned whether it was what I truly wanted. Not once had I considered what another life might be like, one where the pollution of Nevertide's politics and scheming wasn't ever present.

Was I shutting out Hazel because I was afraid? Afraid to choose the uncertainty of love – a concept I knew little to nothing of, afraid to hear the scorn and refusal of the only proposition I could ever offer her – in preference for what I knew, what I had been born to do?

Does it even matter?

To love Hazel would be to literally destroy her.

As selfish and beastly as I was, that was something even I could not allow.

ROSE

Another sunny day in Crete had begun, but despite the blue skies and the twinkling sea below our camp, I felt despondent. We weren't any closer to finding the missing people, and the endless twists and turns in the mystery were doing my head in. We now knew of four people who had disappeared from the island: the great uncle of the Bouras family, who were natives to the island; Lily Anderson, a young girl who had been taken from her room at a nearby luxury hotel; and two prominent archeologists who had also disappeared—but we didn't know the specifics of their case, and I didn't know if it was a red herring or not.

I was sitting with Ashley, Claudia and River outside my brother and River's tent when I spotted my father, brother and two uncles—Lucas and Xavier—approaching.

"Corrine and Ibrahim have some thoughts regarding what kind of creature would get through a sixth-story window without being seen," my father said. "We need to hold a meeting."

I leapt up and returned to Caleb's and my tent to find my husband. He was sitting outside it, looking over a map of the island and making marks with a red pen. He looked up as I approached.

"I've been trying to see a pattern between the disappearances"—he waved the map—"but the only thing that's clear is that they all happened near the excavation site—the old man's hut isn't far from there, and neither was the hotel resort."

Reaching down for his hand, I pulled him to his feet. "C'mon. My dad's calling a meeting."

We headed to the center of the camp where we found the rest of our gang sitting among a cluster of rocks, Ibrahim and Corrine in the center. Caleb and I took seats in between two other couples: Arwen and Brock, and Shayla and Eli.

"So," Ibrahim said, crossing his arms as his eyes passed

over the group, "I think we have quite thoroughly concluded that the only type of creature or creatures that would have been able to take Lily from her hotel room would have been one that had shape-shifting abilities—to make them very small, invisible, or perhaps take on the form of something else entirely, something that wouldn't be suspicious."

"So we can't rule out fae," Ben muttered.

"Or even ghouls," Lucas added, his voice a tad hoarse as he exchanged a glance with Ben and Kailyn.

"Oh, that's right, Novak." Corrine nodded, a slight smile unfurling on her lips as she eyed Lucas. Like Kiev, Lucas was another man whom Corrine had a penchant for winding up whenever she got the chance.

"Nor must we rule out some kind of creature that could tamper with memories," Ibrahim went on, "either erasing them completely, or persuading someone that what they *thought* they saw was something else entirely..."

Ibrahim was cut off by the loud ringing of my father's phone. My father stood up and pressed it to his ear, his face growing more serious by the second.

"Hm," he murmured. "Yes. Okay. We'll be right there. Do ask the family not to go anywhere." He hung up and looked at us. "Another lead," he announced. "Another person missing—a woman, a mother. We need to head to the Kostas Plaza."

Everyone hurried to their feet and gathered around the witches present among us—Shayla, Mona, Corrine, Ibrahim, Brock and Arwen—before they vanished us from our camp.

When the ground became solid beneath our feet, the location we'd arrived at took my breath away. The place looked like a palace, a vast place made from beautiful domes buried into the hillside, with countless gardens and swimming pools dotted about. This family was obviously wealthy, like the family that had been staying in the luxury hotel.

The witches keeping up a spell of shadow over us vampires, as always, my father led us to the plaza's entrance. On arriving in the lobby, we were greeted by a bushy-mustached local policeman who looked like he'd been expecting us.

He gave a brief nod to my father and began to explain in a thick accent. "I spoke to the family already. A father and a son, they've been staying here for a week. The mother was discovered missing this morning. She went back to her accommodation to take a rest while the others went to the golf course." He dangled a set of room keys.

"These will get you into the room."

My father took the keys and held up the keys to the group.

"Seventh floor," my mother muttered, eyeing the numbered key ring.

"And let me guess," Ben added, "there's no sign of damage to the building?"

"None whatsoever," the policeman replied grimly.

The witches magicked us up to the seventh floor. On reaching the large suite that was the family's residence, we were faced with complete havoc. Tables were overturned, curtains hanging drunkenly off their rails, and an expensive TV set now sported a huge gaping hole in the middle of it.

"Hm... Where's the master bedroom?" Lucas asked, wandering off.

We—or as many of us as could fit—followed him to the end of a short corridor, littered with glass from frames that had smashed along the walls. When we entered the bedroom, we were met with a similar sight—clothes pulled out of drawers, mirrors smashed, and the closets broken and open.

"Look at this." Claudia was pointing at something on the floor. I peered past an overturned dressing table and saw that a pot of face powder had been spilt over the carpet. Right in the middle of it was a huge hoof print, cut perfectly into the powder.

I almost laughed. "That's the most blatant plant I've ever seen."

"Yeah," my mother muttered, arriving at my side. "These 'minotaur' tracks are fast losing their effectiveness."

"All the valuables appear to be gone," Eli reported from behind us. "Likewise at the Andersons'. The pattern emerging is the targeting of wealthy families, staying at the island's best resorts. According to the research I did earlier, the missing archeologists were staying in a gated villa complex, so they count as another wealthy target. The only one that doesn't fit the pattern is the uncle... Let's all go down to that old beach house."

We made our way back down to the hotel lobby, where my father handed the keys back to the policeman who was waiting patiently for us by the door.

"We'll be in touch," my father told the man before we exited the building.

We stood around for a few minutes, studying maps to see how far away we were from the uncle's beach house. Eli was right—there was something odd about the nature of the uncle's disappearance, and so different from the rest. He would have had nothing of value to take, and was a local resident, which indicated to me that he hadn't been specifically targeted like the others had...which perhaps meant that he'd seen something that he wasn't meant to, or done something to warrant a punishment.

What on earth is behind this?

"Okay, got the location," Ibrahim said. "Gather round, crew. Gather round."

A few moments later we were crowded around the witches again, who vanished us to a pristine beach that appeared to be deserted. The sun was starting to set now, turning the sky a beautiful pink and gold. As we moved along the sand, we spotted our destination: a small beach house at the bottom of a cliff, which looked out onto a rocky cove.

As we drew closer, I realized just how ramshackle the house was—more like a rudimentary hut than anything else. Reaching its porch, my father and Ben moved to the entrance first, followed by Lucas and Jeramiah. The rest of us circled the hut to investigate.

I told Caleb my theory about the old man perhaps seeing something he shouldn't have, but as we walked down to the water's edge and the jetty that backed into the sea, I just couldn't imagine what it had been.

"Hey!" Griffin called out. He was crouching down in the sand about five feet away. A bunch of us hurried over and saw that he was pointing to a set of footprints—small ones, smaller than my hand.

"These are weird," Griffin murmured. "Doesn't look like somewhere that kids would play."

I agreed. The area seemed too hidden away to be particularly attractive to holidaymakers, and the way the sea smashed at the cove rocks made it seem too dangerous an area for swimming.

We followed the footsteps toward the other end of the cove, where the rocks became larger and more cavernous. Soon the one pair of footsteps became a dozen—like an entire horde of children had been marching across the beach.

"Calida and Silvanos had lots of kids," I remarked doubtfully, recalling the niece and nephew of the missing man.

"Uh… were they all the same age and the same size?" Griffin replied, furrowing his ginger brows. "All these prints are practically identical."

We came to a stop in front of a large cave, and this was where the trail ended. Our group—which Derek, Ben,

Lucas and Jeramiah had now rejoined—entered the dark cave. It took a split second for our eyes to adjust to the darkness, a bonus of vamp sight, and then… I gasped. Almost every one of us gasped.

At the back of the cave, jewels and trinkets glittered in great big piles. I took a few steps closer, noticing that some of the objects also looked very ancient…as if they might have come from a museum or an archeological site.

A muffled cry made me jump, and I turned in the direction of the noise.

"What the…" Caleb muttered, as we all laid eyes on five humans tied up against the wall, all gagged and eyeing us with desperation.

"Oh, my…" my mother said faintly.

"We're going to get you out of here," my father said, stepping forward to reassure the humans. He extended his claws—which only made the humans whimper more—before stooping to slice through the ropes that bound them. But just as he severed the first knot, footsteps echoed at the entrance to the cave.

It wasn't any of us. We were all already inside.

"Who the hell are you?" a voice demanded in a high-pitched squeak. A small creature stepped into view, no taller than a five-year-old.

"A fairy," Corrine gasped.

Seriously?

Fairies were something I had never seen before in my life, but had been informed about by our witches in The Shade. This one was a female—her face fleshy and disproportionately large compared to the rest of her body. She was wearing a brightly colored polka-dot dress she'd obviously stolen from someone much larger and her skin beneath it was a coarse, ruddy brown. She had thin white hair that clung to her scalp, while her features were both sharp and round, her ears pointed and nose bulbous. Her face was scrunched up in a hateful scowl.

"A brownie, to be exact," Ibrahim added beneath his breath.

As far as I understood, those were the more meddlesome type of fairy.

Within the blink of an eye, the childlike creature was joined by several more of her kind—four more females and two males. They quickly barricaded the entrance and, hands on their hips, glared at their intruders like an evil kindergarten class.

Well, this could have been a lot worse. On catching Caleb's eye, I had to fight to suppress a laugh.

During GASP's years of operation, we'd had to deal

with a multitude of dark, foreboding creatures. Fairies certainly made for a surprising—and not unpleasant—change.

* * *

We could finally return home to The Shade. After days spent in a tent, it would be nice to be back in the luxury of our treehouses. It would mean that I missed my children more—our house felt much quieter without them—but I was sure that Caleb and I would find things to fill our days with until they returned.

We had arrested the band of brownies, escorted them back to The Shade with us, and stuffed them in The Black Heights in a spare storage chamber where they had been kept spellbound, literally, by Corrine and the rest of the witches. We had to decide what we were going to do with them.

After a brief rest, Caleb and I visited the mountains to see if any progress had been made. We bumped into Corrine as we neared the interrogation quarters.

"What's going on?" I asked her.

She rolled her eyes at me, rubbing her temples. "We've isolated the little white-haired monster from the rest of them, since she seems to be the ringleader." She gestured to the wooden door grimly. "Be my guest."

Caleb and I entered to find Ibrahim still in there with my parents. Sitting on top of the interrogation table, with her legs dangling in mid-air, was the first brownie we'd come across. The "ringleader". Her pink polka-dot dress looked much more distressed than a few hours ago. When she laid eyes on Caleb and me she exhaled with a loud huff of disdain.

"More intruders!" she said crossly.

I smirked, making my way over to Ibrahim and my parents, who sat at the opposite end of the room.

"How's it been going?" I asked them.

They all looked as fed up as Corrine had.

"Well, let's just say we're this close"—my father held up a hand and formed a tiny gap between his thumb and index finger—"to resorting to torture, unless this little liar confesses to her wrongdoings."

"I haven't been telling lies!" the brownie erupted. "I haven't!" She swung her legs in agitation. "In fact, *I've* been kidnapped—taken to this horrid place. You won't even give me food!"

"You have been given food," my mother muttered, "you just want different food than we deem appropriate for a prisoner."

"Huh!" The brownie crossed her arms and exhaled another huff. "I'll not be treated this way! I don't know why you're picking on us!"

"Well, we found the missing humans tied up in your cave," Ibrahim delineated for what I suspected was the umpteenth time, "along with all their valuable belongings, and, of course, the cast-iron hoof model that you used to cover your tracks. I think that sums it up."

"I don't know what you're talking about! I just stumbled on that cave with my friends!" she screeched.

"Oh, really?" Ibrahim countered. "That's not what your friends are saying."

She looked at him with narrowed eyes. "What do you mean?"

"I mean that your friends are talking. And unless you want to spend the rest of your days cooped up in here, you should start doing the same."

"I don't believe you!" she replied haughtily. "I think *you're* the fibber."

"Well," my father said, interrupting Ibrahim and rising to his feet. He gestured to us all to head for the door. "You let us know when you're willing to get out of here... God knows I can be a very patient man..." There was a dark twinkle in my father's eye that told me he meant business;

he had something of a track record for playing warden and locking people up in dungeons... Jeramiah had certainly once experienced the brunt of the darker side of my father. My father had put a freaking ghoul in with him.

The brownie gave a cry of despair as we exited the chamber.

After we'd bolted the door behind us, the five of us broke out in chuckles.

"Well the big scary Minotaur sure was a red herring." My mother smirked. "I wouldn't have guessed it would turn out to be a bunch of brownies."

"You mean a clever and organized theft ring," I corrected.

Those brownies had been smart. All the hysteria and hoopla surrounding the Minotaur had not only attracted more tourists to the area, but it had distracted attention from the theft of valuable items. It was almost the perfect crime.

As we left the Black Heights and crossed the clearing to make our way back through the redwood forests, I took my husband's hand and smiled.

"You know," I told him, "I almost hope those brownies stay tight-lipped—at least until Benedict, Hazel and their friends return. It'll be a quirky surprise for them to return to after weeks of human normalcy… Yet another addition to our Shade 'zoo', as Corrine likes to call it."

Caleb chuckled.

Ibrahim and my parents soon parted ways with us. They continued straight ahead, toward their respective treehouses, while Caleb and I took a right toward ours. We had almost reached the foot of our tree when a female voice boomed through the forest from behind us.

"Hey, Rose. Caleb."

We turned to see Claudia hurrying toward us, Yuri at her side. She was clutching a phone in her hand. Both of their eyes were wide and anxious.

"What's going on?" I asked as they halted in front of us.

"I couldn't resist finally giving Ruby a call," Claudia said, strangely breathless, "but it went through to voicemail. I also tried dialing your kids' numbers as well as Julian's. All on voicemail."

I exchanged a glance with Caleb, then looked back to Claudia and Yuri and shrugged. "I wouldn't be too worried. They're probably out doing some active—"

"We also tried calling the center," Yuri interrupted, his jaw tight, "no answer. The call got disconnected before we even got through. We tried every line they list in the brochure, at least one of which is supposed to be manned twenty-four hours a day."

"Have you spoken to Ashley and Landis yet, about Julian?" Caleb asked.

"Not yet," Claudia replied. "We were going to as soon as we'd found you."

I was already slipping my hand into Caleb's back pocket and retrieving our charmed phone. I dialed Hazel's number first and sure enough, hit voicemail. Then I tried Benedict's. Then Ruby's and Julian's. My fingers admittedly quivering slightly now, I tried the center's lines that I had programmed into the phone. I was disconnected.

"We've already tried multiple times, from more than one phone," Claudia explained.

My heartbeat intensified.

"I suggest you two go fetch Landis and Ashley," Caleb said to Claudia and Yuri, a step ahead of me. "We'll meet you outside the Sanctuary—we'll ask Ibrahim or Corrine to give us a ride to Murkbeech to check out what, if anything, is going on."

The couple nodded, eyes still gleaming with worry, and took off.

Caleb clutched my hand and squeezed tight as the two of us began racing toward the witches' temple. I guessed my husband's gesture was meant to be a reassurance that there was probably nothing to worry about. That Murkbeech was probably just having some technical difficulties with their signal and phone lines—it was a remote island, after all.

But if it was something more... I swallowed hard, wishing that I had given in to the urge to call my children days ago, when my instincts had dictated me to. But it was too late for regrets.

I squeezed Caleb's hand back as the forest ground slipped away beneath our feet, as the wind ripped past our ears—my reassurance to him that if it was something more, we'd get to the bottom of it.

In true Shade fashion, no member of GASP would stop to breathe until we had.

Epilogue: Sherus

It had been nearly two decades in human years since the battle between the fire fae and the ghouls of The Underworld; it had raged for a day and a night – but in my memory, where the screams of the fallen seemed ever-fresh, and the helpless bodies that fell were burnt into the back of my mind, the battle had seemed eternal.

Looking out across my kingdom from the throne room, and the peaceful, sleeping gardens of my court, I should have been marveling at the opulence and wealth of my people – wealth that wasn't just material, but spiritual too – the result of many years of peace; of children growing up with both their parents, of knowing harmony between all of the fae kingdoms.

In a few moons, my son was set to continue this peace between the elemental kingdoms. He would be marrying Elirara, the enchanting daughter of the water fae king – thereby solidifying the two stars' alliance. The earth and air fae had always been cautious allies, but I had no reason to suspect that the ongoing relationship there wouldn't continue to be as beneficial to us both as it always had been.

And yet.

There was something…something I could feel in my bones, deep within my being, that told me to be alert – to be cautious. To not accept the serenity at face value.

The door to my throne room opened.

"Brother," Lidera's voice melodically floated over to me, "for days now you have stood at the window, watching the stars. What is it that you're hoping to see?"

"It is what I'm hoping *not* to see which concerns me," I answered. My voice to my own ears sounded weary.

"More imagined threats?" she replied, moving to my side to join me at my window vigil.

"The stars are uneasy," I said. "I am not imagining that."

Their configuration in the sky seemed too close, too

bright – their normally, pure white light seemed waxy somehow – yellowed. It was a sign.

"Oh, Brother!" Lidera laughed and nudged against me. "We have weakened the Underworld ghouls, our pact undone…what other threat would there be to us? Can you not just admire the fountains – look at them,"—she pointed— "they bare the sigil of this house in celebration of your son's union with Elirara. This is a joyful time."

I looked down at the fountains. In our kingdom, they were created from white-hot fire, not water – their shapes licking upward toward the night's sky. They ensured that our land was never in darkness, that nothing could ever hide.

"Do you imagine, Sister, that because it is beautiful now, it must always remain that way?" I asked.

She shook her head, but merely laughed again, refusing to take my words seriously.

"You are too gloomy, Sherus."

"And you are burying your head in the sand," I countered. "Not for the first time."

She sighed. "Will you ever forgive me for abandoning you? It has been years – and I have tried to make it up to you."

I already regretted my words. I'd given her too hard a

time for abandoning me when we weren't meeting the quota of ghosts that the ghouls required. It was cruel to keep hold of such a grudge, especially with my sister; she was sensitive and quick to hurt. And, I reminded myself, it had not been her pact – it had been mine. I was right to bear the brunt of the responsibility on my own.

"I apologize. Forgive me, Sister."

"Forgiven," she replied, patting my hand in reassurance. Her joy at the forthcoming nuptials had made her more easy-going than I'd ever known her, and she had been warmer toward me than she had in an age. I shouldn't spoil it.

"How is your friend – the one who walks around in the body of a fae?" she asked curiously. "Have you heard from him?"

"Benjamin Novak? No. I have not. I assume all is well in the human dimension for him … I have not heard otherwise."

"You gave him a great gift, Brother."

"The gift was his," I retorted swiftly. Benjamin's help would never be forgotten, but I considered us even. The young man had been able to rejoin his loved ones – a chance at a second life. Few of us were that fortunate. I had not gained as he did from our exchange. I still mourned the loss of the oracles who had needed to die in order for our pact with the ghouls to be undone. Had the sisters still been alive, my unease would have been proven or quietened by their knowledge. Without those twins, I was second guessing threats, trying to understand the unfolding of the universe by myself – a foolish ambition.

"You have gone again, Brother," my sister smiled up at me again, teasing. "What are you thinking of now?"

"The oracle sisters. They are a great loss to our people."

"They were horrid if you ask me," she murmured. "I am glad they are gone. I never liked them, nor their strange brand of magic." She shivered, and turned away from the window.

"I have to help with the wedding preparations," she informed me. "I am journeying to the water kingdom, I won't be gone for long. But eat, rest – be your best for the wedding, Sherus. That is your only kingly duty at present."

She left, her silken slippers padding across the gleaming topaz stones of the floor. I crossed the room, determined to stay away from the windows for a while. I had introduced a recent levy on the rarer stones in our kingdom, and there were a few disputes that needed my attention. I had a servant summon my chief treasurer to me and we sat around a table to discuss.

We had only been sitting for an hour, however, when I was interrupted again – by the sound of the emissary's soft whistle, a sign that he was waiting outside my door.

"Enter!" I called out, placing my parchments down.

My best emissary, Jida, stepped into the room.

"What news?" I asked, negating any pleasantries – there would be time for all that later. Right now I wanted to know the latest news of the other elemental kingdoms.

"I am pleased to report that there is none, your highness," he replied without expression. "All of the kingdoms are truly pleased about the upcoming wedding, and all the kings are unwavering in their desire to see harmony remain across the four stars. You are highly regarded, your highness – the days of your father's rule long forgotten. They see you as wise, as benevolent. I have been looking for five days and five nights, and I have not come across a soul who wishes you or your people harm."

"And within my own kingdom?" I asked sharply.

"The same. The people are wealthy and over-fed. No one desires to see that end," Jida replied.

I nodded.

Perhaps my lurking sense of unease had been my imagination all along. The over-active imagination of a world weary king who saw veiled threats everywhere he went…I sighed.

"Thank you Jida. You may go. Return to your family, I may need you again before too long."

He nodded curtly and left the room. Then, wanting to be alone again, I dismissed my treasurer, too.

Breathing out, I leaned back in my chair. The two people I trusted most in the world—Jida and my sister—had just told me that I was wrong. That my instincts had been incorrect.

But even so, my unease wouldn't vanish. Though the night was still, and all appeared to be well within our four stars, I could not escape the feeling deep within my gut that told me all was not as it seemed. That in some distant place, a danger was stirring… Awakening. A danger from which no dimension would be safe if an army was not prepared to fight it.

READY FOR THE NEXT PART OF THE NOVAK CLAN'S STORY?

Dear Shaddict,

Thank you for continuing the Novaks' journey with me :)

The next book in the series, _A Shade of Vampire 36: A King of Shadow_, releases **November 30th, 2016**.

Pre-order your copy now and have it delivered automatically to your reading device on release day:

Visit: www.bellaforrest.net for details.

I look forward to seeing you again very soon ☺

Love,

Bella xxx

P.S. Join my VIP email list and I'll send you a personal reminder as soon as I have a new book out. Visit here to sign up: **www.forrestbooks.com**

(You'll also be the first to receive news about movies/TV show as well as other exciting projects that may be coming up!)

P.P.S. Follow The Shade on Instagram and check out some of the beautiful graphics: @ashadeofvampire

You can also come say hi on Facebook:
www.facebook.com/AShadeOfVampire
And Twitter: @ashadeofvampire

Made in the USA
San Bernardino, CA
12 November 2016